Jackalope Hunting

Also by David Hancock

Dewpoint

Jackalope Hunting

David Hancock

5119, LLC

First published in the United States in 2009

This edition published in 2023

ISBN 979-84-303634-44 (paperback)

Titles, margin text, and front matter set in Century Gothic

Running text set in Garamond

Contents

1
Grand Canyon

I am a sojourner. I am a runaway. I have decided to find a new home, settle where the money runs out. Now I am states away from all I grew up with, looking for dinner, and finding what my grandfather saw in Arizona. He used to tell me about it and how he grew up wishing to go from there to Vermont, Washington, or anywhere with seasons and changing colors.

Until five days ago, excepting a fishing trip with my grandfather, bi-annual family reunions on Curacao, Saint John, and other islands, I had never left suburban Chicago for more than a weekend. Now, without air conditioning, I've driven through six hot states. Today has seen almost ten hours of driving. There is a striped, bunched beach towel on the seat and my legs stick on an uncovered strip of black vinyl. My car is a 1977 Plymouth Volare Roadrunner, Spitfire Orange, and, at twenty, is two years older than I and filled with so many rust holes he has won the name 'Colander.' Road wind moves through his front seat, rustling maps pinned under the arm rest. Traffic ahead kicks dust into my face, heavily freckling my sunglasses with a crystalline patina; my hair is gritty and dry. Overhead, ferret-, saucer-, and trident-shaped clouds cast shadow spots on the desert.

At a Grand Canyon scenic view, I stop, parking between some white vans and two motorcycles. The only rivers I have ever seen are the Chicago and Mississippi, which are both fairly turbid. The Colorado's hues look like the sky after sunset. Around me, a group of students studies the river and the canyon's features, tracing lines, curves, and faults with their index fingers. They discuss what the layers tell them about advancing and receding oceans. On my other side, a couple with their arms around each other's waists follows the horizon with their eyes, in unison. "You can see so far," she says.

"It's unreal." The canyon is full of color: green, reds, and the river's blue. It has levels and spires, and looks far less like a canyon than I had expected. Around the scenic view and in the parking lot is the desert's rust-colored sand. Wind moves it in strides across open spaces and under parked vehicles.

The group, students and chaperones, takes pictures and an older, smile-creased man whose remaining hair is gray names rock layers. Tired from driving, I rest against a fence for a time, put a foot on the higher railing and press down to stretch, listen to the breeze rouse bushes and speak its moving language. This is a nice view, will make for nice pictures to remind me I was once here. Eventually, the students file into white vans labeled "Topeka Community College, Topeka, Kansas" and drive off. The couple gets on the motorcycles and leaves.

Colander's trunk is tricky and unpredictable. I turn the key in the lock, jiggle it, but the lid doesn't open till I hit the trunk while turning the key far to the right. Inside are two duffels of clothes, my father's garment bag with my suit inside of it, a rolled sleeping bag, a flat pillow, and a large, black, industrial plastic camera case. It is eighteen by eighteen by twelve inches of air-, dust-, and water-tightness. I undo twin combination locks next to the clasps. Inside are my Nikon F3 and six lenses as well as thirty rolls of film. I fit the camera with its telephoto lens, setting it in the bayonet grooves and turning it counterclockwise. The clicking into place feels important; the lens, having turned in my hands, slows then is ready to extend sight. Through the viewfinder the canyon comes closer, focuses, unfocuses, clarifies. Shrubs, once distant, cone-ish things, become twisted, branchy, adorned in thin, rough leaves. They edge near the Colorado, two frame the broken prow of a wood canoe. I take ten photos, careful to frame the pictures with objects of interest to pull the viewer's eye toward the centermost, most important, object. When I put the camera back, the removal of the lens is a mini-death to any unborn pictures here. This camera represents three nights a week of jockeying register at a convenience store for two years. It is the most valuable thing I own and the only possession which I have had to save for then buy a piece at a time.

After putting the camera back, closing the case, locking the locks, I sit on the sun-warmed towel covering the driver's seat. Sun hits my face; through closed eyes it is red. I turn the key backwards and listen to talk radio. There is still an hour's drive until my campsite and dinner. It will be the first meal I have eaten, since before I left Chicago, not pre-wrapped in plastic or sold next to a cash register worked by semi-mannish women. A length of duct tape on the passenger's seat peels up. Smoothing the tape glues my fingers. It peels up again.

I turn the key forward. Colander ratchets and exhales to consciousness. Leaning on the wheel, feeling the hard vinyl burn my arms, I look out one last time at the canyon. "What do you hope to find, Merak?" It is my father's voice, close as if he were in the car. "Answers? Let's hope not." Regardless of what I find on this trip, or new life, or whatever it is, leaving was the right decision.

The tape's glue makes the steering wheel tacky. Colander's tires make and pull a low cloud of dust behind us.

‹◊›

For dinner I stop at a fifties-style greaser. The parking lot is rutted, light gray gravel starkly different from the Martian-red around it. There is a sign above a blue and white striped awning which reads "D IGHT D ER." There are dark outlines for the missing ' AY L IN .' A black-haired girl sits on a stool at the counter, her arms on the white surface, leaning towards a small TV with half a bunny ear antenna and a fuzzy image of a news anchor.

When I enter, a cow bell hung so the top of the door strikes it clonks. Cold air hugs me inside and my skin contracts. The girl turns off the television and sets it behind the counter. She wears a red dress straight out of a Frankie and Anette movie. She uses a green hairband to pull her hair into a

3

pony tail which moves as if guided by overpowering inertia. Her name tag says "Anna."

"Have a seat wherever."

I sit in a booth away from the restaurant's sunny side. She follows me, sits opposite, pulls a menu from the table menu rack and says "Our special tonight is hamburgers and home fries."

"That's your special?"

"Wednesdays are our slow days. We keep the special simple so we have less to thaw."

"Makes sense. I'm really in the mood for a pizza, though. And a pitcher of Dr. Pepper." I order a large with ground beef and hot peppers, even though I hate peppers, but Anna recommended them. In the kitchen Anna takes a pizza from the freezer, unwraps it, adds toppings and sets it in a stove. Her hand lets go and the door slams shut. When a tall, thin man with a hairy, beach-ball belly walks, palm-to-forehead style, from somewhere and begins talking to her, Anna looks at the floor, nods and apologizes.

I walk to the bathroom, a fuscous room with a cracked sink, a wall of peeling paper, cracked plaster behind it, and a dingy mirror. I splash water onto the mirror and the dirt trails off. With my hands I wipe more off then rinse it again, drying it with crunchy toilet paper. I wear a dust mask, darker along my hairline and temple. My hair is the color of the desert. In the sink I rinse my face and arms, run water through my hair. Reddish water drips to the sink or floor, peeling off eleven hours of road. I splash water on the sides of the sink to clean the dirt, then wipe my face and arms with paper towels from a loose roll set on a hand dryer without an on button.

When Anna brings out a pitcher of pop, I say: "Join me."

"I really can't."

"There aren't any other people here."

"My dad – but," she glances at the kitchen, "he's not paying attention." Anna gets a glass for herself and sits opposite me. "There's a cute face under all that dirt," she says.

"I've been driving all day and got kinda of dusty, I guess."

"Why not use your air conditioner?"

"It's busted, has been for like fifteen years. I never remember it working in this car."

"My house doesn't have it either. But here does. That's one reason I work so many hours, I suppose."

"Good reason."

We sit and sip our pops quietly.

"We gotta talk about more than the A/C," she says. "What's your name?"

"Merak."

"Interesting name. What brings you out this way, Merak?" Anna puts a straw in her cup and drinks through it, leaning down rather than lifting her glass. When she sits upright I see she has chewed her straw into mass of white bends, like I do. "You sound like you're from Chicago."

"That's creepy."

Anna shrugs. "I meet people from all over the world here."

"I just needed some time away from my parents. But I don't plan to go home. It was hard to leave, but now that I'm away, I think it'll be easy to stay gone. For me and my family."

"Why?"

I shrug. "How about you? Ever left?"

"No."

"What about for college? When do you go?"

"I graduate high school next year and plan to go to Tucson for biology. I want to come back to here and inspire young Indians to go out and make a name for themselves. But tell me about where you're from."

It is not with shame that I sigh, but apprehension. Deer Lake, Illinois, is a village of decently sized, vastly overvalued homes with above-average plots. "I can sum it up pretty quickly. My neighbors have matching his and hers BMWs. They leave them out Saturdays to show off."

"His and hers?"

"That's what the license plates say."

Anna giggles. Her eyes close, head angles forward, and she covers her mouth. "Are you serious?"

Nodding: "You're cute when you giggle. Well, even cuter." My neck involuntarily spasms. I would never say this to a girl back home.

My friend Amy, she's gorgeous. A bit too thin, but she has this long blonde hair that, when she leans backwards and props herself up on her elbows, the tips of it skate back and forth across the grass, or her bed, whatever she lies on. Amy doesn't talk like a pretty girl, or walk like one, she keeps her face down and her body covered. Anna does not. Anna's near black eyes are up, level with mine; she talks freely, as if discourse is little more than a rehearsed parley; her dress is short-sleeved and hemmed at her knees; her socks are pulled up and folded down, the mouths just above her ankle bones. Anna is used to being the pretty girl.

From the kitchen there is a buzzing; the pizza is done. Anna stands to get it. Around the restaurant there are ten tables, a handful with all four chairs, and fifteen booths, five to each wall. All the booths have juke box ports. The front counter lines the wall perpendicular to the door back to the kitchen, and is lined with sparkling blue padded stools. The windows have Venetian blinds in alternating blue and white, except one where a repair placed two whites next to each other, the concentric lines disrupted. Anna sets the pizza on a metal cooling rack a few inches high. From her apron she pulls a pizza cutter. "How big do you want the slices?"

I want to stuff half of it in my mouth at once. "Small, please," because I don't want to seem rude.

The wafer-thin crust cracks under the cutter's wheel. I unfold a napkin and set it on my lap. It is a detail I almost always forget but, when I remember, try to make look instinctual. I pick up a square piece of pizza from the corner, the edge of the crust still hot and when I touch the sauce with my finger it burns.

"It's sweet of you to say that I'm pretty. Do you tell all the girls that?"

I suck my finger to calm the pain then say "No, no I don't." I blow on the pizza slice and look at Anna seeing what she will say.

"Don't you know any pretty Illinois girls?" she sips through her straw, her lips parted just enough I can see her incisors work the plastic.

"I do," I say then take a tentative bite of the pizza. I push the small bite to the side of my mouth and say "lots, in fact."

"Then are you flattering me to get me in bed or because you'll never have to see me again?"

Crust scrapes as it goes down. I table the pizza and hold my hands up, as if blocking a mauling. "I'm not trying to get you in bed, honest."

"Well, good for you." Anna refills her drink by tilting the pitcher sideways. Ice splashing in spills some Dr. Pepper. I dab it with the napkin from my lap; a side of it turns to a brown swamp in the spilled pop.

"What do you mean I'll never have to see you again?"

Anna leans back, pulls her hair from its pony tail and runs her fingers through it. She picks a lost strand from her shoulder and with clockwise circles lets it drop to the floor. "A lot of guys come in here, truckers, tourists, and they're really sweet and nice and everything and most admit they never talk to girls at home like they talk to me."

"You must be something special, Anna."

"Do you like jokes?"

"Yeah," I say, thrown.

Anna rubs a finger on her temple. "There's these two woodpeckers, Merak. One Alaskan and one from Texas. They're at this woodpecker convention in Texas and they're talking. The Texan says 'we have these Ironwood trees and none of us can peck into them.' He then goes to an Ironwood tree and pecks at it and his beak gets all bent like in a cartoon. He straightens it and says 'See?'. The Alaskan asks for a try and bam-bam-bam pecks right into it. 'Why – that's amazing,' says the Texan. 'We have frozen trees in Alaska. This was nothing.' So the next year the Texan woodpecker goes to visit his friend in Anchorage. And the Alaskan shows the Texan a frozen tree and pecks at it and his beak gets all bent. He straightens it and says 'this is why your Ironwood was no problem.' 'Let me try,' says the Texan. He goes up to the tree and bam-bam-bam pecks right into it." Anna did not look at me as she told the joke.

"I don't get it."

"The moral, Merak, is that the further you get from home the harder your pecker gets." She looks at me, waits for something. I don't laugh, don't groan or say 'I get it.'

"Usually people laugh when I tell a joke, even a dumb one. You really aren't just after me, are you?"

"No, I'm not. Who are you that all these guys go for you?"

"I'm just a girl who waits tables in her parents' greaser. I'll tell you what it is." Anna leans on the table, a finger lightly back-and-forthing the edge. "There's no rejection guilt. If you ask me out and I say no, Merak, that's okay because you'll never see me again. And the answer's a forgone no since you'll likely never be back here. If you ask some girl in your biology class out and she says 'no', then you have to see that 'no' every day for a whole semester or more."

I straighten the end of my straw enough to drink. "That's true," I say from the free side of my mouth.

"You don't ask many girls out, do you, Merak?"

My face warms upwardly. "You seem to think you know an awful lot about things, but you're wrong more of the time than you think you are."

"That's a no. You probably like a lot of girls, don't you, Merak?" She leans closer.

"Some."

"More than some. Your face is redder than mine." Anna's words touch my face, wrap around my lips and nose, moving across my cheek. She winds her pony tail through the green hairband until the longest tips poke out to her left. "See, I'm right," she says, leaning back, slapping the table and pointing at me.

The pizza sits there. I eat a small slice whole, crunching the crust, and forget about the hot peppers. My mouth pays for it. I fan my hand and suck air through O lips, grabbing my pop, too. Anna looks down, holds her hand to her mouth, and giggles. Missing the pepper to see her giggle was worth it and, when I can talk, I say so.

I imagine Anna and I in a house, with kids. We aren't like my parents. I see us in college, too – meeting between classes and sleeping in each other's dorms. She sits on my bed and does bio or chem and I lie next to her working on government or French. When she bends to pick up a sheet from her folder I turn her textbook page, as a prank.

"Hello, Merak, still here?"

I shake off the images. "Yeah, I am. Sorry. It's just been a lot of driving today. Tired, hungry, thirsty." I look at her again, but it's like I'd never seen her before and this new Anna, different Anna, seems less like a waitress on a slow night and becomes an actual, tangible girl with a future beyond here and a life outside, worries and hobbies, friends and maybe an ex who dumped her when she kissed and nothing more. Anna's lips are level, her eyebrows raised. The look backgrounded by a slant of dust-imbued sunlight; beyond that the counter and cash register would be blurred, the cowbell a nondescript dot. "I want to take your picture."

"Um, okay, I guess."

"I'm sure you're used to it," I say, standing.

"Not really. Once a year for yearbook is all, really. Pictures have always seemed like control to me, a way to capture someone – to keep them like they were then. But they never are like the photo again."

"I understand, I think. But it's a good way to keep memories, too. Memories fade faster than photos. Just remember what my photo teacher used to say; posing for a photo is just like life: Smile and you'll do fine."

"Alright. Should I just sit here?"

The light slant dims and disappears. "How about outside?"

Anna looks at the kitchen. "I don't know, I mean my dad, he might not like if I left."

"It won't be three minutes, I promise."

Anna looks at the table then stands. From Colander's trunk I get my camera and put the macro lens, one which is good for very close photos, on. Anna stands in front of the drawn blinds. Her right wrist is in her left hand and the union hovers at her waist. She straightens her dress and holds her wrist again. "Just like that, good. Now smile."

The first picture is Anna standing, all of her. The second is closer, just a bust shot. She smiles thinly, lightly, her shoulders slope. The final picture is an angle, a pseudo-profile of the left side of her face. She looks at something beyond focus.

"I need to go back to work now," she says. "It was nice meeting you." Anna turns and begins walking inside.

"No one's here, though." The camera hangs, bumping my chest.

"My dad always says if I have time to lean, I have time to clean." She smiles at me. "Would you like your food in a box?"

"Yes, please." Anna walks through the door and I follow before it shuts. "Say, Anna, do you work tomorrow night?"

"Yes."

"I'll see you then."

Anna's smile drops some, turns cordial. I tip decently, but decide it is not enough and I give her another dollar. She keeps smiling politely, but holds the extra dollar in a different hand.

‹◊›

I am not sure what woke me. I lie still, bundled in my sleeping bag on top of a picnic table. A hundred-page notebook, plain red with a black spiral, rests on my chest. In it I've been writing my day's adventures each night since I left. The air is cool and a nearby juniper tree baffles the night breeze. The tree, untold crickets, and a distant truck's engine brakes are the only sounds. My eyelashes part. Sleep dust falls away. Above me are stars. In Chicago it's rare to ever see more than a dozen. Once, in Boy Scouts, in Wisconsin, I saw stars and a satellite, but nothing like this. I take my glasses from the picnic table and what my grandfather called "God's own parade" becomes clear. Overhead is a wide, hazy ribbon of stars flanked on all sides and angles by hundreds of lone stars. A slow moving, bright light passes overhead as well as occasional long flashes of light which end and fade like fireworks; maybe this kept him here, even after meeting my grandmother. I lay flat on my back, my arms between my head and pillow, listening to insects and feeling the air move, smelling juniper and watching a few clouds move east as the sky turns from black to blue.

Hidden by distant mesas and mountains, the sun turns clouds to wheat fields. I take my camera and climb the ladder of a nearby van to sit and watch the sunrise. The foreground is a silhouette peak and plateau, the juniper frames the left. I take a series of shots. Some focus on the clouds, others the foreground, some on the fading moon. To kill the roll, I take three shots of my feet dangling off the van, cover the lens and prepare to jump.

Tent zippers begin to sing; flaps open. The tent next to me buzzes and a tall, hefty man in a white tank top and plaid boxers steps out of it. He stretches his arms wide then looks up at me.

"What the hell are you doing on my van? Get off there, you little shit." His voice is breaking timber.

I purse my lips to keep from swearing. I cradle the camera and jump carefully. He stands next to me, a little taller but much rounder and wider.

"What the fuck? Where are your parents?"

"Chicago."

His head tilts slight left as he looks at me.

"No, I didn't run away."

"Uh-huh. Don't you respect other peoples' property?" From the tent a woman says "Let him be, Frank. We have to pack up yet."

Frank climbs the ladder two steps; the van settles left. He touches his hand where I sat. "You're damn lucky it ain't scratched. Get outta here. Don't pull this again, boy."

With the standard 'yessirs' and 'never agains' that come with being let off the hook, I step away. I stow the camera in its case and shut my car's trunk. It pops open. I shut it again, hop onto it. It stays shut. The camera, it strikes me for the first time in the two years since I began buying it, is worth far more than my car. I wonder for a second if Colander can keep the camera safe.

Breakfast is last night's pizza and a vended apple juice on a shaded bench overlooking the gray and fog-bound canyon. The far edge comes and goes as denser clouds move between it and I. It is an apparition.

After finishing the pizza and juice, I let things settle and watch the trail's entrance. There are two rangers wearing press-creased pants and shoes polished to reflectance. They each stand next to a sign. One says "No running, fighting, shouting or horseplay." The other says "No bathrooms beyond this point." The rangers share smiles and 'good morning's with each hiker.

From brochures I picked up at the first rest area in Arizona, I had imagined the Grand Canyon to be mostly sand with some standard desert plants. The scenic view yesterday dispelled that. Here, though, it is more colorful, larger, and vastly deeper. There are yucca and shrubs all over, due to heavier than average rain, one tourist tells another. The plants are rough, haggard with bristles and spines instead of leaves and bark. Though not decorative, or leafy, they have a beauty which stems from their simple hardiness; the sort of beauty which can either make for good pictures or bad pictures. Most of mine will probably be the latter. Lizard tracks move between shrubs, giving the desert a pieced-together look.

When breakfast settles I go to the general store and buy two disposable cameras, three water bottles, and a hip pack with "Grand Canyon" and a stylized crevice on it. Expensive is not a strong enough word for it all.

"Mornin'," I say to the rangers. The man smiles more than does the woman, whose hair is a pencil-speared, tan-blonde bun. I imagine she drives close to her steering wheel, the sun visor permanently down so she can easily reach the CDs pouched there.

Ten feet down the path, hex bolted to the canyon wall, is a yellow on brown sign:

ABSOLUTELY NO LITTERING

OR THROWING ANYTHING

 INTO THE CANYON.

A piece of purple gum, still glistening like a gem, is in the middle tine of the "E" in littering.

Immediately around me are maybe twenty tourists. Some speak German, some French or Spanish; a few speak other languages. An Asian couple walking ahead of me stops every thirty or so feet to take a picture. Stop, snapshot, go. Stop, snap, go. Stop snapshot with wife on rock, go.

Periodically, I, too, stop to take pictures. The last remaining clouds are being pushed out and eviscerated on spires. The path twists around itself like a stretched spring. Inside the corners and along the edges is a constant till of gravel and pebbles. I kick them a little and want, more than anything else at this moment, to sit and throw a handful into the canyon one at a time.

A third ranger, her red hair pulled up and hidden under a hat, sits on a bench down the path. She wears lip gloss and talks to tourists.

"I start about four a.m. I hike down to the mid-point station with two other rangers. We open it and check first-aid kits. Then about fifteen minutes after we open the trail I just hike up and down for six hours until it's time to go home." She pats the first aid kit held close to her as she talks to a man with his son.

The man, holding his fidgeting child's hand, says "so you're an EMT, then? I'm a fireman, myself."

"I'm sort of an EMT, not really. I'm trained in first aid and CPR. If anyone faints or passes out, which happens a few times weekly, I get there first. Some people try to do this hike with too little water, or come from lower elevations and don't realize the air's thinness here. And of course some people just aren't fit enough to do it. Last week we had to airlift someone out who was too heavy for all five of us to carry up. She had fallen and broken her ankle near the mid-point station."

"Wow, really?"

"Yup."

The father tugs his son's arm a little. "Did you hear that? They have a helicopter."

The boy, who holds a stuffed cat, kicks a piece of gravel into the canyon. "Okay."

"Don't you want to know about it?"

He shakes his head and walks behind his father's leg, holding the cat so it can look out at the canyon.

Now I understand; the father is flirting. The child a prop. My own father did that countless times, using me as a prop, a means to show his 'delicate' side, his 'compassionate' side; the side the chicks would dig. Only he also used his money, his car, his looks.

‹◊›

Where I am now, a camera and a half gone, a bottle of water empty, there is a small shack with two rangers. Surrounding it are a number of benches and flat rocks lining a large, flat area blasted into the canyon wall. People sit on the rocks and benches, resting; I sit and lean against a wall that looks like a cross-section of corrugated cardboard. Though I have never been here it is familiar to me like someone you meet after having seen them on television. I absently rest my elbows in two of the half-circle grooves. There are no outhouses, no water pumps. People stand at the shack asking the rangers questions. How old is the Grand Canyon – the bottommost rocks are 1.1 billion years old or more; the canyon took around 200 million years to carve. Do rangers make good money – the job's rewards are in helping people enjoy the canyon. And, with a frightening sincerity, "Who built the Grand Canyon, people or Indians?"

The blasted-out area is cooler than the trail. A large white dial on the side of the shack has a needle pointing just under "85." There is another in the sun with a needle pointing between "95" and "100." I arrange my hip pack with the empty bottle on the bottom and the cameras on top. Up trail, people descend in a procession. Some move slowly, others pass the sightseers in a hurry to make their turnaround points more quickly.

Though free of clouds and fog, I don't see the canyon. I see, instead, Anna. She sits in a bedroom like Amy's. Anna looks at herself in a white-framed mirror with pictures of her friends wedged in the frame, and runs a candy-colored brush, the sort a child would have, through her hair. Around her are unlit candles scented vanilla, jasmine, and forest. Behind those are collage frames of pictures. Written on them in green marker are "Thanksgiving", "Friends Forever," and "1993." Music plays softly in the background and she has a four-post queen bed. She hums as she moves the brush.

Deer Lake is like any suburb anywhere. The men pay to have companies manicure their lawn so it may be the greenest, or densest, or most even in hue. Our annual neighborhood picnic has door prizes and sizable gift certificates for the house with the best yard, best landscaping, most showable pet. There are tag football games for autographed sports memorabilia. It is just how everyone lives in what I've seen of the world. But I don't see Anna having a lawn, or playing tag football, or even living in a subdivision with annual picnics. But she must, so how did Anna turn out so differently? There is a hand on my shoulder.

"Day ain't coolin' any." It is a ranger. "You been sittin' here a long time, son. Everything okay?" His eyes scan my face up and down, scurry left and right. His hat is in his spare hand and his forehead shimmers like wet pavement.

"Yeah, just daydreaming is all. Getting ready to go back up."

"Okay, just wanted to make sure." He looks into my open hip pack. "Conserve that water. The path back is ten times harder than the path here."

Before I began, I set my watch alarm for ninety minutes, a near impossible goal since the descent took two hours. I'm not sure how long ago that was, though. The path up is ten times harder. There are more tourists, more sun, and more hotter, drier air – the kind that turns sweat to grit too quickly for it to cool. People talk loudly about the size of the canyon and how deep it is. Every bench and flat rock has people resting, dripping water on their foreheads, wiping their faces with their shirts. At one rock two people enjoy its sun-heated warmth. A man has a hand on the woman's belly. "When did you find out?" 'Two days ago.' "How are we going to pay for its college?" 'That's eighteen years away, Roland.' "Will we have to get married?" 'Good Christ, why not just ask if it's yours, too.'

I stand past them to keep their view open and listen to them talk about money for diapers, a crib, private schooling and clothes. He asks who will be with the baby at night since he has to be up at three each morning and can't be up all night if he's going to be cogent on the air. I put myself in his shoes and my gut turns double. I try to understand what my parents felt when they found out about me and I can't imagine having a child I don't want during my last year of college.

The examples of parenting in my life haven't been perfect, but they did teach me that it's a two-person job. And even with all the right decisions they made, here I stand on the edge of a trail into the ground, staring into a giant chasm in the earth, trying to figure out what my life and past means and how it affects my future. What edge will Roland's child stand on when it is eighteen?

In my neck a hollow pain begins and spreads into the base of my head. I drink one of the remaining bottles of water. Some of it splashes around my mouth and, though warm, feels cool on my face as it pulls off dust and drips to the path. I take pictures there of the canyon and sky, clouds that seem to stand on pillars and a thunderhead supported by a column of rain.

When the sun moves between clouds it beats my arms with a whip. Everyone's shirts are dark at the armpits and down the backs. Two men in front of me sweat from their crotches to their collars with dark lines running down their shorts legs, too.

Perhaps my greatest flaw is the absolutely wrong-headed belief that I can do anything without giving it much thought. I may be saying this out loud, or not. I find myself acting out body language as if I were speaking. Were I to think about the future ramifications of my present actions, would I be more cautious?

The two men don't turn around to look at me.

And through this the canyon sits there. Were it thinking, it might consider us weak. Not just us, but all people. We come and pass, see it and move on. We sweat, fall, need rangers and helicopters. It sits there, has always sat there, slowly deepening, watching, judging, unchanging to any of us. Drinking my last bottle of water, I look up; a half mile of trail and nine hundred vertical feet remain to the trailhead. I lean against a wall, the sun angling down on me. I put the empty in my hip pack and pull out another, trying to salvage a last drop from it. The hollow pain of dehydration spreads into my shoulders and down my left arm. "I don't want to be airlifted out of here," I whisper. The sandstone wall presses into my back. "I'm going to make it." The hands of my watch won't tell what time it is or how long until the alarm sounds. "I can do this."

"You can do this," says one of the men sweating, inseams-up. His accent is thick, Nordic.

"I can do this shit. This canyon is nothing to me." I push off from the wall, powering past them, nodding, and continue up the trail. My sweat stings my face where I shaved this morning and the crevices of my nose. After a few more turns, my shirt damp and heavy, I take it off and tie it around my head. My chest and upper arms approach translucence in places. Veins shine like mapped highways. The heat, the sun, the air all take their turn raking my back, telling me the canyon has won, that I cannot do this shit.

Five bends till the top, the steepest section of trail, people begin to sound distant. My stomach rotates and blackness creeps into my vision. Trail grit digs into the back of my knees, and in the seams of my underwear, scraping away at the skin where my legs meet. Walking hurts on my left heel. There is a blister, and it's big. At the next bend, a hairpin left, my ankle rolls and I fall, hard, oofing onto a rock. The canyon becomes two shrinking dots and tunnels and lots of flashing white lights in the darkness. From my back and chest a warm coziness spreads and I stop fighting, begin to dry heave, and wait to pass out.

Someone behind me says 'drink' and that he has water. A bottle appears. I drink. It is so cold my forehead splits open. The water tastes like nothing I have ever had, like my mouth is in a Canadian mountain creek somewhere, and my tongue is unsure of what to do. I drink a third of the bottle and my vision clears, people's voices come back and I hear them asking the man about me. Had I fallen a foot or more to the right I would have fallen down the canyon as the empty water bottle did.

I dry heave again and fight to keep the water down. When I sit, I begin to pull embedded pebbles from my chest. The man asks if I want more, that he has plenty. I shake my head and try to say no thank you.

He is a stocky, box-car man with a wide-brim straw hat and a blue, leaf-print shirt. Above me I hear the rangers at the entrance. They warn people to reconsider descending the trail as the day has become unexpectedly hot. My head is hollow and I hold it, trying to steady the world.

"I've really got plenty. You can have this bottle."

"I'm okay, but thanks." The climb is something I need to do on my own. As I sit there the man watches me to make sure I am okay. The canyon is different now than earlier. There are more colors, more shadows, more points of photographic interest. It is not so different from the autumn my grandfather yearned for, though this change must happen daily.

When I stand, the world feeling a bit less steady than I expected, my alarm goes off. He wishes me luck and heads down the trail. At the top I go to an information booth and lie on a cement sidewalk in its shade. I pull out my last disposo-cam and hold it out in front of me, arm's length, and snap a picture of myself. There are five shots left. For a moment I line up the information booth, just as I see it now with the strands of a plastic straw and receipt bird's nest poking out from where the eaves meet the wall, in the viewfinder but decide to save the pictures for another hike. I lay, watch the nest, wait for the hollowness, nauseousness, and occasional dry heaves to fully pass.

‹◊›

Shortly before dusk, the greaser is full and through drawn blinds the sun is slow-moving cords of light brighter near the kitchen. Anna wears pig tails and sits opposite me so she can see her customers. "If they wave then I have to go. I have to check them once in a while, anyway."

"That's fine." I drink from a glass of ice water in front of me then say "It's interesting, those beams of light." At the holes in the blinds where the cords pass, lines of light slant through and to the floor, parallel, casting a row of white dots across the room like perforations.

"Yes," Anna reflects. "They, I suppose, luminesce."

"Luminesce," I say, thinking about the word. "That's a good word for it."

"You were limping when you came in. Are you hurt?"

"I hiked the Grand Canyon today and have a blister on my heel. A bad one."

"Let me see."

"Your customers, they'd be kinda grossed out."

"They won't notice."

I slide my foot out of my shoe and take my sock off under the table then set it next to me. My foot rests sideways off my knee and I turn. The blister is the size of six laid-out quarters. It's dark red and puffy.

"That's a really bad one. You'll have to lance it." She reaches out to my foot and touches the ball of it. "You have the softest feet of anyone I've ever met."

"That tickles."

She pinches the arch.

"That didn't tickle." I smile contentedly, not showing teeth, to let her know I don't mind. A relaxing tingle moves from my abdomen down my legs and up my back. "I didn't realize the hike would be so rough."

"It is. I've done it a few times. A number of different hikes. Which trail did you do?" Anna takes her hand back.

I turn and put my sock and shoe on. "I didn't see the name of it, but it had a ranger station half way down."

"Ah, okay. That's the big tourist one. It's pretty easy. I usually do the hidden ones. Those trails, when you hike them and it's just you and the canyon, those are the ones to take. The canyon walls there, the rocks have more random patterns, become murals of a sort. At one place there is a bison in the rock, at another a city skyline. Other places have other forms, wrestling arms, an ocean wave, things like that. Plus, the canyon is very different when it's one-on-one. More dangerous, but more intimate. More like a lover who's hurt you and apologized and, though you accept it, know he will do it again."

"I don't know what you mean. And I definitely won't go into untamed nature. Especially alone. It'd be too easy to never be heard from again – there's no trusting nature."

"I don't know about that. I think there is." She taps the tabletop. "That's not a curse, perhaps, what you said about not knowing what I mean."

Anna sips from her drink. "You had a more interesting day than I did, at least." Anna tells me her day was the "same thing as always. Lunch rush, dinner rush, dead afternoon. Tourists, a lot of foreigners. But they make up most of our business so that's okay." She looks past me. "I'll be right back." She walks toward a table of three Asian couples. I do not want her walking away from me. There's a specialness to someone you don't want to see leave, my father once told me. More, of course, than someone whose absence is welcome and far greater than someone whose leaving you are indifferent to. When he said that, it didn't occur to me to wonder which role my mother filled.

Between tables, Anna is lone movement among exhausted tourists idly nibbling finger food, recouping from and recounting their days' activities. Anna takes an order from the six people at two pushed-together tables and after a few minutes comes from the kitchen with a tray of beer, pop, water, and appetizers. Her walk is petite steps and I imagine the heels of her shoes wear through first. My arms rest on the table and I look at the fried cheese sticks I lack the energy to eat. My foot, sore from touch and confined to a shoe, cancels any plans for a hike tomorrow. Instead, reading and treating my foot with various topical ointments sounds like a good idea. When Anna sits back down she sighs and her knee cracks. I ask why she wants to teach.

Anna tilts her head up and left, runs a finger over a pig tail. She looks at a coffee stain ceiling tile as if reading it for an answer. "I want to give other Indians a chance to leave the reservation. You don't realize what a blessing it is to be able to go of your own volition."

She asks about my hike and I tell her about nearly passing out and almost falling and how my head swam in a thorough, acute pain.

"We have the highest suicide rate of any race. Did you know that, Merak?"

I stop, try to see the connection. "No."

22

"John Richards and Rachel Bennett jumped into the canyon, not together. Charles Running Cloud blew his head off after killing his parents."

"Why?"

"Why do we have the highest suicide rate or why did he kill his parents?"

"Both."

"Same reason. We have no hope. Highest unemployment rate in America, lowest education level, worst schools."

"You seem to know a lot, though."

"I'm lucky to have worked here since I was twelve. I've gotten to know about the outside world more than some." Anna's head tilts up and left. "I want to teach biology so that I can show Indians that there's a place they can have, that there are jobs they can do. By teaching biology I can interest people to become doctors, scientists, and vets. Some will come back to the reservation to also help inspire; others will go out into the world and make a bigger name for themselves. It's all about breaking from our past."

Twenty background conversations have a warbled, rolling, laggardly drone.

"How do you break from your past?"

"Ah, finally he asks it! 'How Indian are you?' I knew this would come. Well, I'm as Indian as someone can be living apart from other Indians. I see them at school, but don't hang out with them; I work too much for it. I don't wear feathers, or paint my face, or hold any traditional beliefs; I don't even know anyone who does."

"That's not what I was asking."

"What were you asking?" She leans toward me, resting her chin on her hands.

"I meant your own past, really, nothing cultural."

Anna sits upright. "Oh, well, that's a whole other question. No one's ever asked that. I don't have an answer."

I bite a mozzarella stick and sip water. "I've never known anyone who killed themselves. I can't understand why someone would."

"Even if you lived here your whole life, Merak, you could not understand it."

"Hey, Anna, no one's perfect." I hold my hands open to her.

"That wasn't a cut, Merak. It's not good, bad, or indifferent – it just is. Be glad for it." She slides her fingers back and forth across the table top, slowly, her thumb under the edge. Her fingernails are shiny and short, without cuticles.

"You spend a lot of time filing them so they're all even."

"Don't change the subject. Look, Merak, you're a nice guy. Guys like you fall in love with me all the time. Guys like you, they want to be my rescuer, my white knight, to save me from the evil dragon that is this restaurant. Well, this restaurant isn't a dragon, isn't evil, you're no white knight, and I won't be falling in love with you, Merak."

"I'm not in love with you."

"Not yet." Anna sips the water in front of her and wipes her lips with a napkin. "I need to get back to work. Tomorrow I'm off." Standing, she says, "don't ask; the answer is no."

"At least I won't have to see that 'no.' "

Anna, facing away, stops and looks off to a corner, then begins walking again.

On my way back to the campsite I stop at a small gift shop and buy two books, one a book of stars and how to read the night sky, the second an espionage novel by someone I've never heard of. At the campsite I unfurl my sleeping bag; it rolls out like a carpet at an event. The lining looks like tree bark, the outside a simple drab. I lie on it much of the night, letting my heel air, applying peroxide, reading my book about the night sky.

I, the middle point between the zenith and nadir, eventually lay with one hand behind my head looking for constellations listed in the book. I find Pegasus, Waterbearer, and Capricorn as the slowly spin.

Soon, however, the book is on the table's bench and I write in my spiral about the hike, the corrugated cardboard wall, the rangers and Anna in Amy's room. I asked Anna about how she breaks from her past, personally. I think we both know how I break from mine: running. But she didn't know how to answer and the more I think about that the more I suspect everything she tells me is scripted. All in all she's afraid I'll fall in love with a bunch of stories. What worries me is that I someday could. Not her and her stories, but some other girl and some other stories and that when I realize my mistake it will be too late. I sharpen my pencil with my Swiss Army knife and log in my blister. I draw a flat-ended oval in the middle of the page to show its size. When I close the notebook, the pencil marking the next blank page, I let my eyes close.

The kitchen doorframe is missing a door. Anna, in a dark blue tank top and cut-off khaki shorts with frayed legs and a hole on the left cheek, stands a few feet from me, facing away, doing dishes at a sink. The tap is on full, steam comes from the water as it exits the faucet. Anna looks out a window facing a white cement parking lot with eight cars and two empty spaces with intersecting lines of grassy cracks. Beyond that is a sleepy little road and a stand of red and gold trees mazing through old, boxy homes.

Anna reaches into the sink, into a blue plastic dish bucket and pulls from it a white plate with an intertwined red and gray border. She scrubs it with a sponge, rinses, and sets it in a drying rack on the left counter. Her hair is in a French braid below her shoulders with a blue rubber band holding it in place. I walk behind her and reach around her waist, into the water, for a second sponge and a dirty plate. The water is smoggy and suds are rare islands. There are more plates submerged, and forks, too. In the corner a trash can is a piled with spaghetti on top of junk mail.

I kiss her clavicle and twice down her shoulder before she pulls it away, rinsing the dish and saying 'Maybe later, or not. Flowers, an I'm sorry, and help with dishes is not an apology.'

'I know. But I am sorry.' I rinse the plate and set it in the drying rack. Water sheets off it and into the plastic tray below. Seconds later a waterfall forms from the tray to the sink.

'You don't understand.'

'I try.'

'The refrigerator broke again.'

<〇>

In the morning I read my espionage novel for a while then take fingernail clippers from a duffel. I sit on my table with my leg level. No one watches so I cut a hole in the blister. Thin, red fluid squirts out. I work the trimmers in a line to the outside of the blister then around it, letting little pieces of my foot fall into the sand. Wind and dust burn the raw, exposed heel. I fill the cap of my peroxide bottle with the clear fluid and drip it on the wound. It foams and stings, demonic pain rings and throbs the outside of the blister and runs hot pokers over the middle. I lie down and hold my forehead, squeezing to overpower the pain in my foot, letting the raw skin air.

<〇>

I drive slowly into the greaser's parking lot, avoiding ruts. I pull next to a white and wood Chevy pickup with just as many rust holes and amateur Bondo jobs as my car. Anna casts the doors of the restaurant open. The cow bell clonks as she exits. For some reason I am surprised that Anna is not off work tonight. She has on green jeans and a white shirt under a red apron. She pulls the apron over her head and tosses it to the gravel. For a second my heart beats a good fastness, feels as if it has its own life, dreams and desires. I imagine her opening her arms as she runs. No slow motion nor music, just a hug. She will ask to come with me wherever I am going. I step out of my car and face her.

"You just don't get it, do you?"

"What?" My heart beats a bad fastness, feeling inside like decay. I shut my door gently.

"I don't want you coming around here, Merak."

"Why not?"

"Because you'll fall in love with me. You don't understand my life at all. You just don't get that I don't want you near me." She walks around my car and stands by the passenger's door.

Holding a shrug, I say, "Who said anything about falling in love with you? Besides, this is the only place I know for a good dinner." I set a hand on my roof but it burns. I pull it off, smacking my thigh with it just to change the pain. "Besides, Anna, I really like you. You're not like anyone I've ever met." There is a hand print on my roof where my hand had touched.

"Why do you like me? Do you think I'll just fuck you?" She stands next to my car and points at me, staring me in the face, slapping the roof of my car with important words. From her pocket she pulls a one dollar bill, holds it and waves it in front of me then tosses it on the passenger's seat. "I don't want your charity."

"That wasn't charity. And you're just not like anyone I've ever met."

"I'm exotic? Like some bird of paradise or strange animal?"

Palm prints cover her side of Colander. "No. You're incredible, fascinating, and I just want to hear your stories. You almost told me one, last night, when you had to answer something no one had asked, when you couldn't give me a choreographed reply."

"Open this door."

I get in my car, reach across it and let her in. We sit there and look forward at the sun sinking behind an abandoned railroad switch house a few hundred yards away.

"You want a story?"

"Yes."

"Here's my story, Merak. I was born inside the Grand Canyon by a midwife who was drunk and stoned. I'm lucky I'm not paralyzed or retarded. My father is an alcoholic who keeps telling us he's hit rock bottom and stops drinking. But all it takes is a slow month at the diner, a change in land laws, or – like this last time – his cousin marrying a white man, and he starts in again. He can drink a half gallon of gin a night. Or a case and a half of beer. He goes out for days and then comes back. And he's out there screwing whoever, drinking whatever, and the money he spends could buy me a bed or blinds. All I have in my room is a flat mattress, my sheets are my drapes, and two cardboard boxes. One is for clean clothes and one for dirty."

"I didn't know." Anna's face changes. I had not seen her do anything but smile and suddenly, as she tells me this, she is old and tired. Her face limps on her skull and her hair is knotted at the ends and dry. Other flaws I had missed show, too: a stamp-sized blemish of lighter skin on her left cheek, a few hairs above and under her lips, a semi-circular scar on her hand which she had picked at when she mentioned her father's drinking. They remind me of a saying my photography teacher used: Imperfection is the playground of beauty.

"You couldn't know."

"I'm sorry."

"I hate 'I'm sorry.' It means whoever says it can't understand."

For a moment I want to tell her my family is not so different, about my parents and why I won't go home. Behind me, my father's voice tells me to be quiet. It has enough authority that I do so. It says to listen because I am about to hear a story she has never told, one not fabricated.

28

"My family, I have a huge family, disowns one of its children a year, sometimes more, for marrying white men or women, Merak. And when any man of another race comes in and my father sees us together, he gets angry."

"Does he hit you?" I say though the voice says not to.

"No." The switch house is dour with two rays coming through the windows. "I want to leave, Merak."

The voice adds 'now' and tells me to start the car, drive away, and forget about the diner.

Anna and I sit. Her hand rests on her leg and I reach over to touch it.

"Parts of living out here are great. I do love my family. I have this land, and what it means. I know my place. I don't ever have to wonder where I came from or who I am. It's a gift, not having to ask those questions."

"I had a dream about you last night. We did dishes and looked out a window at a parking lot and a road. It was quiet."

"What does that have to do with anything?"

"I thought you might like to know." Her jaw flexes and slacks; she looks forward. "It would interest you," I say.

"Don't kiss her," father's voice says, "stay where you are." I take Anna's hand and kiss it, then reach behind her head and pull her in, kissing her lips. For a moment she kisses back.

Then she changes. Anna pulls her hand back and gets out of the car, slamming the door shut. "I've thought about it a lot, Merak. A lot," she screams. Anna slaps the roof of my car in timpanic bursts as she speaks. "I was lying in the heat of my parent's trailer, on my mattress, lying there thinking about you, Merak. And how un-fucking-fair it is we can never know each other."

I watch her hit the roof.

"You get to go back to your big house and big lawn and neighbor's matching BMWs. But you do knowing that truck," she says, pointing at the

29

white-and-wood rust beast next to me, "is the one my dad's had since he was sixteen. His family saved up to buy it, his whole family. They thought he could use it at college, get off this land and do something. He had a four-year baseball scholarship." She pounds the roof of my car with both hands, over and over, faster until her hands move at different speeds and sweat beads on her nose and lips are knocked free by her exhales. The Volare's trunk pops open, just then.

We walk to the back of the car. Her eyebrows and lips shake, a smile being fought. I try not to laugh and cry and yell at how cruel the situation is. She looks inside at the folded luggage, holed canvas duffels, the old sleeping bag, flat pillow, and generic tool kit and says "I expected nicer things. Maybe we aren't so different." The she sees it. The black camera case and the two combination locks.

"What's that?"

"Just my camera."

She touches the case, leaving trails of dust, feeling it as she would the first time she touched anything unknown. "This is a big case if it's just for the one you used the other day."

I dial the locks, each of them open with 35-, for the third of May — my birthday, 13-27 the four digits of my address. Inside, tucked neatly in the pluckable foam rubber interior are my camera, black and shining new with just three small scratches, two flash attachments, a 500 millimeter lens, a 250 millimeter lens, a 105 millimeter lens, a 24 millimeter wide-angle lens, a 55 millimeter lens, a 30-80 millimeter lens, and a 100 millimeter macro lens. They are all Japanese-made and ringed, at the foam's edges, by three dozen rolls of high-end film.

"How much did this all cost?"

"Around forty-five hundred or five grand, a few hundred more if you include the case."

"And the film?"

"Another couple hundred."

"So you're going to be a photographer? Are you out here learning your trade?"

"I'm not good enough to do it for a living."

Anna tells me to step back and closes the trunk so forcefully the back of the car dips. She puts her hands on the spoiler and rests her weight. "That's fifty-five hundred dollars in photo equipment – for something you're not even going to do professionally. My parents' trailer cost less than that. That's more than eighteen months' work here." Anna rests her forehead on the trunk, sighs and shakes her head. When she faces me again her forehead is a dusty oval.

"You don't get it. We're different, Merak. You'll go back to Chicago and to college somewhere. You can't hide that from me. In time, you'll never again think about me and when you hear the name Anna you'll think only of a faint idea that at some other time you may have once met another girl named Anna but you'll never place me. Go home, Merak, do good things with your life if only because I can't."

"What about Tucson, and teaching? Showing Indians what they can achieve. Those speeches, are they just speeches?" Why must everything be a speech with people? "Is all you've said just something rehearsed a thousand times on a thousand tourists?"

"Most of it. People want to hear it; you want to hear it."

"Those speeches won't last you forever – Anna."

"You want to hear we're picking ourselves up and how being concentrated on reservations wasn't so bad because we still have all the opportunities everyone else does. And it just isn't true, Merak, it's not true." By the time she hits 'everyone,' she cries. She looks away and her crying sounds something like laughter but she runs the back of a hand up her cheeks. "Merak, you're not broken enough for the desert. Go home, where you belong." Tears held tense under her eye reflect the red of the evening's last direct sunlight. "Just go." She mouths, "go."

My car false starts twice then ratchets to life. I grab the shifting lever behind the steering wheel. It burns my palm. I let the pain course through my hand, arm, and into my head, enjoying the calmness well-deserved pain can have. I back out and Anna stands next to her door. It is unlocked and I look at her. Ahead of me is the road and I go to meet it, driving away from her. Anna shrinks in my mirror, dust obscures her, and soon even the diner is gone.

◇

During the next sunrise, clouds are kneaded apart and rejoined, but there are no pictures to be taken and looking at my camera and the trails of small hand prints on it makes me queasy. I set the rolled bag and pillow behind the camera case and slam the trunk. I open it, struggling and pounding the top, just to slam it once more. I imagine Anna sits atop her trailer, or perhaps on the steps, and looks to the northeast or the nearest road. Perhaps she sleeps or does what she can to forget me. Or maybe she has forgotten me like last week's heartburn.

Though my reservation has one more day, I cancel it. As much as the idea of maybe going home sits uneasily, I suddenly want the trip to be over and my life to fast forward a year so I don't have to make any of the coming decisions about college and life.

There are a lot of things I will never know about Anna, such as if she waited for me to turn my car around after I left. All I can ever know is that before I leave the Grand Canyon I place the towel on my seat, the maps in the glove box, and drive shirtless through the desert, the windows down and my car going sixty-five or faster.

2
Monument Valley

After telling my father that my mother was cheating on him, he gave me this speech: "Merak," he said, his voice slightly deeper than normal – it is usually an octave deeper than mine, "you're going to college in the fall. Don't make the same mistakes I did, so listen well. In high school I was a ladies' man, same in college. I partied, drank, I got girls to match me shot for shot and faked being drunk to make them think they were 'safe' to go home with me. I did a lot of things I shouldn't have. When I was your age, I'd had seven girls under my belt. I spent high school and college spreading legs, son. That's how it was and I'm saying it straightforward because you should know and there's just no candy-coating this. Most every girl I've slept with, I regret. I shouldn't have done them, er, it, I mean. Look, Merak, you've already been a better student, better person, than I was at your age. And I'm proud of you for it." I looked at his face and wondered, at forty, would worrier's lines describe me from forehead to cheeks and neck, too? Old pictures of him are mirrors, with bad hairdos.

We were in his Saab, going home from the Chicago Antique Car Show, an annual trip since I was six and old enough to start learning about cars. The older, closely bound condominiums and apartments of the inner suburbs passed us. A brown 1950's-era complex with a green pool and white asphalt parking lot had a sign on the roof which said 'If you lived here you'd be home by now.' These buildings gave way to the silver glass offices and sound-dampening walls of the outer suburbs.

"There are three things men in our family pass to their sons," my father said after minutes of quiet. He held up a fist and began counting them off from his pinky in, while he slowed for a toll plaza. "We all sneeze like our father. We all look like our father. Since at least my great-grandfather, all of the men in our family have ended up married because they knock some chick up." He reached into the ashtray for change, counting out forty cents in dimes and kept his gaze forward, toward red lights and our line of cars, not even routinely checking the mirrors.

"You should know, Merak," he looked at me and tapped a finger on the dash, change jingled inside his fist, "that I love you very much. I never loved your mother, though. I just don't. She doesn't love me, either."

"You used to say it to each other."

My father looked back to the road ahead. "It's important to keep up appearances. For you, the neighbors, especially the church. That gets hard in time, though."

The car felt like it listed far to the side and I leaned on the window to counter. Nothing. We moved forward some. Two men in a truck next to us laughed, heads back, mouths open, eschared lips. One probably said 'that is so true, so truuuuue!' The car moved forward and father rolled the window down, humid-hot air sidled across the leather seat and around my forearms. He tossed the dimes into the toll basket and accelerated us into our seats.

"Don't get me wrong, son. It could be a lot worse. Your mom and I have a good arrangement. It's cheaper than divorce and we both still get ample time with you. We don't hate, or even dislike each other." He shrugged, gestured his right hand in a carefree, politician's way. "But don't make my mistake." He pointed his finger at me like a minister in fire-and-brimstone mode, raising his voice to a damnation-sermon level with important syllables. "Don't get married just because you get a girl pregnant. Get married to a girl you love – then get her pregnant."

"How'd you meet mom?"

"Don't do this to yourself."

"I'm not."

He looked at me. "You're so goddamned melodramatic. You're worse than a woman sometimes."

"Thanks, Dad, that makes this so much easier on me." I wiped a finger under each eye because, after years of him stressing the importance of being masculine, decisively manly, stoic and predictable in my emotions, he had erased all I thought about myself as a man.

"Geez, alright, Merak. We'll do this your way. But I've been here. Questions won't make this any easier on you – if anything they make it worse. There are a lot of things that shouldn't be questioned. Damn. Okay, here's how it happened. Your mom lived in the dorm next to mine. It was our senior year. We met, of course, hit it off, and she had you the day before commencement." He paused. "We never even went on an actual date, per se. I wish I'd taken her to dinner a few times back then, I guess. Gotten to know her, or something." He looked at me. "You're taking this too hard, son. I know. I've worn your shoes, sat in that seat," he pointed. "My father told me the same thing in the living room of our house when I was your age. Told me in the room we'd had Christmases and Birthdays in for eighteen years. None of them should have happened." Father bit his lip. "You must not do as I did, as your grandfather did, as all Snyder males have done. My father warned me, as I am warning you, do not get a girl pregnant before you marry her. Having a child is the most wonderful thing you'll ever do, but right out of college it's hard. Too hard." He tapped his foot under the clutch pedal. "That said, I'd not change a thing about it. Even marrying your mother." He shifted into fifth gear and used the shoulder to pass a car in the left lane. "I'm sorry about what I said. I didn't mean that thing about you being worse than a woman. You're not."

"Would you still have married mom if she hadn't been pregnant?"

He turned the radio on to a conservative talk station. "No."

‹◊›

35

I arrived at Monument Valley shortly after dark last night. I spent the day driving from the Grand Canyon here and stopping at roadside gift shops. They were all similar with their carved malachite eggs and pyramids, quartz bookends, geode halves, petrified wood clocks, rocks glued to cards, and mass-produced dream catchers. After checking in, I sat on a picnic table and recorded the day in my journal then read more about the night sky. Far off, a freight train sounded its horn and the locomotives accelerated, their generators powering up. On hillsides around the camps people walked, stooped low, carrying ultra-violet lamps and following spiral patterns outward. They hunted scorpions to sell as pets at roadside stands. The small, far more lethal ones could fetch good money. In the morning the hunt's focus changed from scorpions to tarantulas, the campsite's owner explained.

"They move around looking for exotic insects to sell. They spend a few days somewhere then move on to another place, it's an annual cycle. But they stay on public land; they're real clear on the lines of the national parks. Taking an insect off park lands is around twenty years in jail." He is old, Asian. The hair across his head is thin, patchy in spots. His beard is the same, as are his teeth. His skin is liver spotted and the ones on the sides of his face stretch and relax as he speaks, but his clothes are pressed and new.

"Isn't that dangerous?"

"About one a year dies, maybe more, who knows; no one really cares. At least one dies, though." He writes a bill of sale for me. "It'll be fifteen for the night."

I hand him a twenty. "Can I get five in quarters for the 'Laund-Ro-Mat'?"

"That won't get you two loads. It's two and fifty for the wash, fifty for the dry."

"Damn." I set another dollar down for change. "Soap?"

"There's a machine in there. Takes dollars. The red stuff, blue stuff, the other blue stuff, and bleach. Dryer sheets, everything."

"Hey, if you don't mind me asking, what brings you out this way? You don't strike me as the standard sort of Arizonan."

"Utahan."

"Ah." I expect him to have some ancestral connection to the railroads. In school I did a paper, basically parroting class notes, about the heroic contribution the Chinese gave to early Western railroad construction. It got an 'A-'.

"Border's pretty moot here, so it don't matter. When I was about thirty my wife and sons and I were thrown in an internment camp. Lived in Portland before that. That was during the second one. America did that. Same as the Nazis, only we didn't slaughter interned people, just kept them in the desert. Same thing, really, no gas needed. All of us were Japanese."

I am disappointed in myself for mistaking his nationality.

"My wife killed herself with a broken drinking glass, slit her belly from side-to-side — hara-kiri." He demonstrates the motion then counts quarters into stacks as he talks. "Two of my sons died of exposure, the third in Germany. The government buried them out here. So I stay here to be near them."

"Oh. I'm sorry. I can't even begin to understand."

"It's been a long time. No harm or foul in asking. I don't mind people asking." He holds six four-quarter stacks and slides them from his hand into my two cupped hands. "If you'd like to hear about the internment sometime, just let me know." He shuts the register, looks down at it. "This country is still a good place," he watches a car pulling a long cloud of dust park, "but only because the good has shared bath water with evil." He pauses, seems to think about an afterthought, then adds it: "It's important we not forget what we've done — as a people or as individuals."

"Next time I'm out this way," I say because 'no' is too rude, too dismissive. And because they hadn't taught us about internment in high school. Shock, surprise, and doubt all fight for predominance.

From my car I take the duffel of dirty laundry and wash the heat-cured stench of bacteria from it. Behind the glass doors of the Clean Machine 2500s, the blues, greens and grays of my clothes tumble and mix with white-turning-tan suds. Two children climb on the driers, jumping off only to climb again and try to push the other to the floor. Even children try to destroy each other.

When the air conditioner kicks on, first a humming then a column of cold air from a circular ceiling vent, I shiver though it is set at eighty. When the doors open and local people come in to the 'Laund-Ro-Mat', dry heat envelops my calves and reminds me it and the sun are patient tormentors.

<0>

Monument Valley appears as little more than a flat red-brown waste populated by scrub and rocky pillars. But it is more than that. A simple glance around shows the trails of various insects large and small, lizards, birds, and a dog. At a tourist rest along highway 163, I stop and get my camera. In the shade of my car I sit and re-dress my heel. When I finish, a strange aloneness comes to me.

Though I brought no one with me, there had always been people around: at rest stops, in Anna's diner, in the campsites, the 'Laund-Ro-Mat'. Here there are no other tourists, no hikers, no families ending summer break on a high note. And perhaps most unexpectedly: no cars, no tires on pavement, no trucks' engine brakes, no distant trains ramping up or slowing down.

—Nothing—

In the shade of my car, the wind moving like the ocean in conches, my body ready for the sun, heel ready to walk, the gravel and stones, sand, and small, lost pieces of plants needling the tender skin behind my knee, I stand, pulling myself up on Colander's open window frame. The hike to the far side of the nearest pillar is an hour. There, in the shade of the campanile-like pillar, I sit, spilling warm water on my head and shoulders, soaking in the air's coolness, and taking in a desert that makes the idea of Wiley Coyote falling into a mushroom of dust next to me seem possible. Under a seeding yucca a large red grasshopper sits, watching me.

Slowly, I put my arm above the grasshopper, creeping the shadow to and over it. The insect has its last chance to escape. It does not jump; it wants to be hunted. I lower my hand. Its legs move and its carapace opens a split. Quick, I strike my hand between the blades of the yucca and pinch its wings. The hopper struggles to get free and holds a drop of black spit in its mandibles. I bring it to my face, look at it, turn it left and right, appreciate the varied and complex red hues. Illinois grasshoppers are green, and not often this large. They are locust in more than form and eat the leaves of garden plants, lawns, and trees. There are less, now, than when I was a child. I set the hopper on my knee. It drops the spit there, spreads its wings and flies thirty feet to another bush.

I take a beef jerky stick from my Grand Canyon hip pack, tear the wrapper open, and shove the plastic in my pocket. I bite the meat like a general with his cigar and stalk the grasshopper.

June: A week after graduation. I skipped work to go to a movie and there was my mother, with someone – not my father – holding his hand and touching his shoulder as she laughed. I never saw his face. He was my father's height, but skinnier. His hair was fading on the back and he wore a tweed blazer. He took my mother, spun her around, hugged her with his front to her back, turned her without letting her free, and kissed the corner of her mouth as her eyes closed and she seemed to let him carry her full weight.

She did not see me, or Rick when he put his arm across my chest and pointed. He and I and our other friends watched her and the man walk from the concession counter, sharing a bucket of popcorn and a pop, to a large cardboard standup of a coming blockbuster. They pointed at it and he made fun of the action hero's pose. Rick grabbed my shirt collar, popping stitches, and pulled me outside. The four of us went to the parking lot and I sat on the trunk of Rick's Taurus while he got pops from a vending machine. I let anger, betrayal, and everything else root in me. Rick handed me a can but it dropped, bounced off the bumper and hit the pavement. I knew the feeling.

I pinched the bridge of my nose, pushing it until it hurt, trying to feel something else and kill my friends' "man, this sucks,"

"I don't know what to say,"

"Maybe they're just friends,"

"Did you not see the way he kissed her?"

And, "dude, this sucks."

Four weeks. Four weeks' avoidance of family time ended with the car show. At home, Father pulled his car in behind Colander, inching up to the bumper, even though the middle garage door – his door – was open.

"Your mother's good about that, making sure everything is ready for me when I come home. I didn't realize until she went on vacation once how much she helps out. When you get married, never take your family for granted."

Finally, in the driveway, after listening to someone on the radio complain about NAFTA, he looked at the steering wheel and sucked his upper lip; it sounded like my car does when I steer too far; he rolled the windows down and set his arm on the window frame. For all I heard, the squeaking could have been the only sound in the city. Past him, four Mexicans worked the neighbor's yard. Their names were Jose, Jose, Pedro, and Diego. No one else on the block knew this. Jose and Diego rode mowers in a steadily shrinking oval and the other Jose and Pedro carried gas weed whackers around the house and plantings. Diego waved at me. Children in the street rode their bikes. Mom walked out of the garage carrying knees pads, a bucket, trowel and a garden claw. She waved and smiled. Dad waved back and, grinning, said "wave to your mother, Merak."

I did not.

"Wave, goddamnit."

I did.

Mom set the pads on the grass by her row of rhododendrons. She looked down at them and back at us, curious and perhaps worried. Perhaps she knew, or not, that the time of 'the conversation' had arrived; either way, she put it from her mind and knelt, pulling English ivy by the roots.

"For eighteen years I've worried about the day you'd ask me this, or the day I'd have to tell you."

"Why would you have to tell me and, wait, you know about him?"

"Yeah. His name's Brian. Nice guy, actually."

"How can you be cool with this, Dad?" I'm sure I shouted that because he rolled up the windows and told me to stay calm.

"You don't need to worry about your mom's and my affairs." He winced at the word. "Bad word. Sorry, I meant your mom's and my business."

"You know about this, and you're fine with it, and you let mom have this affair?"

It hit me. The speech about genetics and accidental children. I knew when he said it that I was his accident, the only reason he and mom were married, but knowing is not understanding.

"First, it isn't an affair if the other one knows. Second, it's not so bad, Merak. I mean, I was a mistake, my father was a mistake. Not being in love with your wife does not mean you do not love your children. My father, just before he died, once told me that this Snyder family tradition goes back further than he ever knew, past his father, perhaps. He didn't know for sure; he didn't get along so well with his dad."

"It's an heirloom." I knew, though I did not tell my father this, that he and grandfather had also not gotten along.

He rapped the steering wheel with his knuckles a few times. "I've always thought we get along well. I hope that was anger, not you, speaking." He reached down to the ashtray and fiddled with some change, acting as if he counted it. "This only has to be a catastrophe if you make it so. There's no reason for you to hate us because of this. One day you may have to tell this to your son." He sucked air in a Vivaldi tune. "I don't envy your position, but am old enough to recognize that you're not unlucky to be here. How you deal with this will speak greatly about the man you will someday become. I did not handle it well and that's been reflected in who I am ever since.

"Don't think of this as an 'heirloom,' Merak. Heirlooms are creepy desks and shitty netsuke cabinets, chintzy porcelain statuettes or collector plates with images of sloops. Heirlooms stay around, collect dust, serve only to constantly remind you of those dead – this does not have to. You can end it." Something in the tone of the 'can' was imperative, firm that he wanted to say 'You must end it.'

I opened the door and ran out. Mother stood, playing tug-o-war with a long vine. I took my bike and pedaled like I was trying to stop my own heart. In my imagination my father has told her hundreds of times that I knew.

"Margaret, he knows." He may have said. Sometimes he just shook his head. Others she ran after me but he caught her and told her to let me go for now. That I needed to work this out as he once had. Or she'd just know when she saw my face. She'd know what I knew and that it was her fault I did. Mothers just know these things.

After the driveway I rode to Rick's house to tell him I needed his car, but I'd bring it back. He tossed the keys and said okay, without breaking eye contact with his video game. He let anyone borrow his car. It was the third new car his father had bought him that year – people kept totaling them. I went to a bookstore and bought maps from The Mississippi westward, every map they had. I spent hours in a city playground, sitting on a bench watching a handful of parents come and go with their small children and thought of the times my mother had brought me to a similar park. I would stand on a platform with a wheel and play pirate captain, climb the rope ladder to take over the other 'ship' and, when dusk came, the mosquitoes buzzing our ears and noses and mother said it was time to go, I would take a mortal wound and fall 'overboard' into the 'ocean' of recycled radials. I wondered how many of the children there were mistakes, if any, and tried to guess the ages of the toddlers and mothers. Most looked older, later thirties with four-to-eight year olds. The younger ones, nineteen year olds with five-and-six year olds, were nanny's, au pairs, and babysitters.

I planned different trips, dozens of them, tried plans to visit every site I wanted to, but settled, ultimately, on the Grand Canyon and Monument Valley because my grandfather had spoken of them most often, because he stayed in Arizona after his family left, and because it lined me up to stop at his grave in Colorado at some point.

The next day I came home while Dad was at work and Mom was out, perhaps with Brian. I packed clothes into my old Boy Scouts duffels and put them, a sleeping bag, my pillow, and camera in the trunk of my car. On the kitchen counter I left a note.

I need to figure things out before college, like if I'll even go. These are not new questions. I know I leave in three-and-a-half weeks. I'll be back sometime before then. Don't worry, I'll be fine. I'm bringing clothes, my camera, and enough cash to get me through. I know it was my mad money for the coming year, but I'll just get a job. Dad is right, I don't want to be in a marriage like yours. I need to figure a way out of that. I don't want to end up like you two. -M

The house was blue, a light, sky blue that almost disappeared on sunnier summer days like that one. The first floor was brick and the brick had, in places, friends' and my scratched names. On the side of the house, hidden behind a red-twigged dogwood, was a brass plate marking where Tiddlywink, a favorite Schnauzer, was buried.

43

In the front yard a seven-year-old me played catch with a frisbee, father, and Tiddlywink who ran between us trying to catch it, yapping at it as it coasted over him. Father would hold the frisbee at Tiddlywink's level, shaking it, saying 'come and get it' as Tiddlywink ran, then he would throw it just as the dog got within reach. Over that was me at age five, running up and down the loading ramp of a rented moving truck. In the garage my father took the training wheels off my first Huffy and after clicking my helmet gave me a push toward the end of the driveway and my first unbound freedom. More from the last fourteen years layered over the looping images which had already begun. Soon nothing was individual, no memory stood apart from the others, every one was cascading, colliding, mixing like a negative exposed and re-exposed without being advanced in the camera.

I did not want to go. Home was safe. I could sack up and face my parents, go to college and clear my head there, or continue the destiny. I knew if I was to make the most of my time away, if I was even to make the trip, I would need to find something out there, a way to change things. One memory stood out from the rest, then. It was 1994, just after spring break. I took a stack of envelopes from the mailbox. The junk mail I dropped in the trash and there, near the bottom of what I held, was a letter to me addressed in my grandfather's handwriting which, as he aged and Parkinson's took hold, began to look more and more like the tracks of a headless bird.

Before leaving, I went inside, took the letter and an unused notebook from my bedroom desk, pulled my suit from the closet, packed them in my father's garment bag, and decided I would stay West until I learned how to end this family tradition.

That day had taken me to a rest area west of Saint Louis and the night saw me sleep in the backseat of my car, rain and small hail knelling the windshield and roof. I lay curled on the backseat under the sleeping bag, watching the headlights of cars pass across the backs of the front seats.

The grasshopper knows the game. When my shadow nears he flies to another bush. At the new bush, with the mid-day sun and dry heat punishing

44

me like an errant slave, the hopper is pinned by a large, light blue wasp. It has an inch-long black stinger which it runs through the grasshopper's thorax. The much larger red bug's legs kick out and its wings flare but it is the last that it moves. It slow-falls to the ground with a final, deft flop. The wasp keeps the stinger in the grasshopper. I take a picture of the insects, on their sides, the tip of the black stinger poking out the far side of the thorax, being drawn in some, held there and withdrawn. The wasp's eyes reflect a hundred angles of the desert, bush, grasshopper and me. One of the hopper's legs twitches. The wasp flies through the bush and away.

«◊»

By late afternoon the clouds have come and gone, grown, puffed like fugu, and rained themselves away. My arms are red, a dark and angry version of Colander's orange paint. I coat them in cortisone then toss my shirt over the passenger's seat back. There are hours to go till camp; the road calls like a kalavinka, the mythical bird that summons men with song and kills them. A bed would be such a nice change.

The West is a place I had only ever dreamt of. Passing Monument Valley, having seen it and the Grand Canyon, I understand why so many artists and photographers have made it their home. Images from Ansel Adams and Georgia O'Keefe recall themselves with key rock formations or shapes. It is here where artists come to try to capture what God did right the first time, Grandfather used to say to me during family reunions. I would go tell my parents, ask them to let us visit, my mother would decline the invitation without a thought or word from my father. She always called Grandfather 'Quentin,' not 'Dad,' as I had heard friends' parents do.

The West is in fact so beautiful that I forget to look at things like how much gas I have and if there's a filling station and after some driving time my car begins to knock, lose power, and coast to the side of the road. I beat the steering wheel with my arms. "Stupid car, stupid, stupid, stupid car. How could you run out of gas on me here?" The towel against the backrest is hot on my skin. Down the road there is just heat-like-water. No signs of gas, no roads, nothing on the maps, either.

'Better the devil you know,' Father often says, and I put my shirt on, take my camera and a telephoto lens from the case, and begin to limp back the way I came.

‹◊›

From behind, a red Volkswagen Thing, rear wells almost to the tires, drives out of the desert like a "B" movie cliche. The backseat is packed with bags, boxes, a hard teal suitcase, and a rolled carpet. A man with shag calves and armpits steps out. His crown of hair is long and black, except for gray stripes on the sides. When he turns I see breasts, very large ones which pull him to a forward lean. It hits me, then, that this is a hairy, bald woman. She reaches down, her bra-less breasts swinging low and stretching the neck of her tank top to give anyone in eye-shot a clear view of long, red-lined cleavage. She scratches her leg and looks at me. She says "young man" in a voice of unoiled metal. "You own the orange car about two miles back?"

"Yeah."

"Need a ride somewhere?"

She is scary. Down the road the pavement ripples and vanishes. "I can walk it." I can do this shit.

"Walk how far? In the desert? Are you suicidal?"

"I need to get gas."

"There's a station about twenty miles down the road. I'll drop you back at your car, too."

"Is it on your way?"

"That doesn't matter." She taps her foot. "Just accept the offer."

"Okay."

"Okay what?"

"Okay, ma'am, I'd like a ride."

She cleans maps, an ashtray, three maple-scented car deodorizers, and a warm six-pack of generic pop from the passenger's seat and places all but the ashtray in the back. She hands me the ashtray. "Mind holding?" I shake my head. "Be a dear and dump it, would you?" The teal suitcase sits against the window and is really an old Smith-Corona typewriter case.

"My name is Watersharer," she says.

"Merak is mine. Were your parents hippies, or something?"

She laughs as she rolls down the window. "I am a hippie. Watersharer was given to me during my first vision quest."

"Oh. What was your name before?" I don't want to talk, or think, just be somewhere, asleep.

"That doesn't matter. Were your parents hippies? Merak isn't exactly a common name."

"My dad's a sports car buff. I'm named after a type of Maserati."

"I see." Watersharer takes a cigarette from behind her ear. She lights it and I roll my window down some. Dry air whips at my face but pulls Watersharer's hair around her, cupping her head.

"Don't see many of these running." I speak.

"Well, Jessup and I have an agreement: So long as I don't sell him, he keeps running."

"Jessup is . . . your car?"

"Yes. He chose the name."

Blink . . . blink.

"Don't give me that look. I've had him for twenty years." She pauses and looks at the dash then up slightly, mouthing words and touching her thumb to each finger in order, over and over. "You're right, Jessup, twenty-two."

The door is unlocked and the thought of jumping is not unappealing.

"I got him after I finished my PhD. Got a teaching job at Oberlin. Ever heard of it?"

I shake my head.

Watersharer inhales deeply through her cigarette and then, after holding the smoke in, exhales out the window by craning her neck like an animal rutting. "Yeah, I suppose you're not the type of student drawn to Oberlin. I taught there a few years then decided I needed to do more with my education. I've been driving around the country since then. I've lived on an Indian reservation, spent some time teaching at some progressive schools in California and New Mexico, and such not." She motions for the ash tray. I hold it out and she rucks her cigarette. "You don't like the smoke, do you?"

"I don't."

She laughs, slaps the steering wheel. "You and Jessup, kindred spirits. I could feel it when I saw you."

The desert passes like a monstrous record. Next to the road, desert scrub plants move too fast to focus on. Far off, a spire stands, nearly motionless.

"You have a good aura, Merak. It means you're meant for good things. Do you know what those are yet?"

I shake my head. "I'm not even sure I'm going to college yet." And you have to get through it without getting a girl pregnant, too. If I could scold my father's voice for saying that, I would. If I knew where his voice originated, which misfiring synapse was culprit, I'd stop it.

"College isn't needed to do good. I've known plenty of people who impacted those around them and never got beyond the sixth or eighth grade. Either way, you should go to a sweat lodge. I did that when I first moved out here. Jessup and I knew Ohio wasn't good for me. It's a spirit-crushing state, Ohio." On the rear-view mirror, three short, frayed tassels; white, red and brown, and blue and green; swing and twist in the breeze. The cords are light, thin, like clean hair. The tags read: 66 for the white, 1974 vertically on the red

48

and brown, and Class of 69 on the blue and green. "Graduation tassels. They used to be longer."

I let them out of my hand and watch ahead of us. Watersharer continues talking about the virtues of sweat lodges and vision quests and how it was in a sweat lodge while living on the reservation in South Dakota that she realized her true calling in life was not in professoring music but in the posthumous teaching of life. She travels to learn about people and how they live. And, in that time, write the longest, most comprehensive book ever attempted on the subject.

"I'm writing the authoritative book on humanity." She thumbs toward the boxes in back. "About twenty-two thousand pages so far. I write three pages a night based on what I learn about humanity that day. Who knows. Maybe you'll find yourself on the pages tonight."

"I can't imagine any greater honor than being immortalized in the definitive work on humanity."

Watersharer either doesn't notice the slight sarcasm, expects it, or is amazingly forgiving. Whichever is the case, she continues as though I hadn't said anything. "All I need is paper, my typewriter, Jana Maaz, the flute and drums in my trunk, and whatever money I get I find or take small odd jobs for. A few months out of the year I teach immigrant kids to read, get a little money for that, not much, but enough." She lights another cigarette and takes two deep inhales off it, craning her head left and blowing smoke out the window through pursed lips. "The Universe, Merak, looks after me. And It will look after you, too, provided you treat It right.

"Trying to walk back to your car in this heat, with one bottle of water, no sunblock, you'd have been found in a ditch picked apart by vultures and coyotes." As an afterthought: "or perhaps not found. You can't beat It, Merak. Cohabitate with It."

The mile markers do not come fast enough. The silence between is clumsy, both of us looking out at the front or sides of the road, anywhere but at each other; it is the silence of someone seeking solitude and someone seeking companionship. "Why did you stop teaching?"

"Academia, it really does nothing to further mankind in any sort of quantifiable way. I needed a life that would get my hands dirty. I have a PhD and two other degrees in music. I could have spent my life studying what makes Orff different from Schuman, Vivaldi different from Verdi, and telling my theories to graduate students, or I could go and do something to improve lives of people who don't have enough money to sit around and talk about why it's significant that one composer favors solos while another changes keys at the same time markers. How does that help people, Merak? If you know, then you see things more clearly than I."

"I don't know. I don't really think I know too much of anything. I don't even know what I want to do when I get back to Chicago or if I want to go back." I don't want to be the subject of discussion. "Why music?"

"Ever the question."

"When did you first know you liked it, I mean?"

"I was twelve. I had taken a detour home from school to go visit one of the museums. At that time I was very much into sculpture. I heard this noise somewhere. I turned a corner and there were these three boys sitting on milk crates and playing buckets, trash cans, and a length of copper pipe, and they had no set plan, no melody, but I could hear in their music, just in the rhythm and pace, the orchestration, a passion for life and a duende, a melancholia, and an enigmatic lostness, too – all this from plastic buckets a pipe. It was just incredible and I saw my life then exploring how music works and what in it makes people feel emotions."

"Then why stop?"

"I started thinking I could figure out what notes and patterns trigger which emotions in people and why – and I could have. But there are some mysteries that, once solved, ruin the puzzle. It's like knowing the magician's assistant is never cut in half, there's just a second girl in the box. And while it can be fun to watch him 'cut' the girl in half, the mystery is lost."

"I don't think many people would know enough about it to have it lost."

"But if even one person is able to see the way the trick works, or the way that music creates emotion in us, then it's too many. Enough of this. You were limping earlier. Why?"

"It is such a long story."

‹◊›

In what I remember of my parents' marriage, they only kissed once. We were at a Dairy Queen in Mundelein. D-Q was a summer event. The one or two family days we had each summer ended at a local diner for dinner then D-Q for dessert. I would order a large Butterfinger Blizzard and end up with a sticky chin and shirt every time.

The night was warm; I remember that because I wore shorts and my Michael Jackson shirt with a screen shot from Billie Jean. Michael was on his toes, knees bent, arms out, the sidewalk lit up under him. The parking lot lamp cast an oval of light around us, lighting the pavement except where I stood. I danced in the light, like Michael, only in reverse, holding the Blizzard with sticky, melted ice cream splashing out the top with my jumps.

'Hey, Billie Jean, keep that up and you might be as good as Michael one day,' said my father. His voice in my memory is round, tunneled.

'And as rich?'

'Maybe.'

'Life would be great.'

'Life's pretty great right now,' he said. Mother and father pecked on the lips. That was it, the entirety of my romantic education.

‹◊›

The filling station's surface has been re-tarred recently. Heat radiates through my shoe and into my heel; the smell of oil spills into the desert. Then the station's glacial wall of frigid air conditioning hits like a sucker punch. The need to vomit rides the back of my mouth like crows on power lines. I ask the clerk where the empty gas jugs are; he points down the middle aisle.

There are one, two, and five gallon red plastic balls with flat bottoms and handles on top. The caps are double-threaded with a valve on one side and a spout on the other; the spout is stored inside, even when the jug is full; the valve keeps gas from splashing out – it's really quite clever. I take a two gallon and ask if I can fill before buying. The clerk says 'sure thing' in a thick, Mexican version of English.

Stepping back into summer heat brings on a headache. It begins above my nose and splits backwards to the base of my skull. I massage my forehead with my left hand and lean against the pump as it clicks the jug full. I turn the nozzle inward and screw the cap on. Inside, I set the gas and the jug on the counter. The store's aisles are packed with opened, half-stocked boxes of candies and beef jerky, road supplies, emergency repair kits, and pre-packaged food. A Twinkie, mashed on one side with cream smeared all over the wrapper's inside, reminds me I haven't eaten a meal today. I grab the Twinkie, a large bottle of water, and a pre-made sandwich from the cooler. I carry them to the front register and, as the man rings them up, walk to the first-aid gear to buy new rolls of gauze, paper tape, antibacterial gel, and Aspirin.

"Seventeen and eight," says the man. His face is a planetoid of pox and acne scars. All the same, it is clean shaven, even in the pits. I hand him a twenty.

"I don't mean to be rude, but how do you shave so cleanly with the scars?"

"You may not mean to be rude but you are."

"I'm sorry. That wasn't my intent."

He drops two singles and ninety-two cents on the counter, on a mat which reads "Born on or after August 10th, 1979? Sorry, no cigarettes."

Looking at the ground, I carry the food and gas outside where I sit and take my left shoe off. I unwrap the reddening gauze and throw it away. I tear open a small, square packet of topical goo and squeeze the cloudy stuff on the wound, using the edge of the wrapper to spread it around the soft, healing skin before starting the wrap on the top of my foot and pulling it around to a comfortable tightness and taping it down. My sock slides on and my shoe, while more bothersome, also cooperates.

The door opens and the scarred man says, "How long you going to sit there?"

Cold air from inside shuttles across the ground and under my legs. "Not much longer. I'll be on my way soon."

"I heard the first time. You no need repeat like I'm an idiot." The door shuts.

The gas station and all beyond it shimmers. I want Anna to walk across the desert, red Annette Funicello dress and pig-tails pulled sideways by the desert wind, alone and beautiful in the heat-water.

Watersharer walks out of the bathroom waving her hand in front of her nose and pulls the handle from Jessup, who is parked in front of the only pump marked "leaded."

She takes a crumpled bill from her loose sock elastic, again showing the world the comb-straight lines on her breasts, and walks inside to pay. "We'll head back as soon as I pay and buy some smokes." I nod and look back out at the desert, at the swirls of sand that move across the land, at the place where just seconds ago I could see Anna walking, see her more clearly than I did when she sat in front of me in the diner. There is just a small spindle of sand rising five feet into the air.

Back sitting shotgun on the hot tan vinyl of the front seat, Watersharer pulls the cellophane off her cigarette pack, smacks it in her hand a number of times while holding the wheel with her knees and turning out of the gas station, then takes the first cigarette out and lights it. I reach down to make sure the gas cap is as tight as it can go, hoping she'll see this and realize the danger.

It plays as a movie in my mind. The camera first inside the car, closing in on the gas can then the cigarette lighter's spark. Then outside showing the car exploding into a ball of rolling flame, the rug, on fire, flying toward the audience and a chassis with four flaming tires rolling to a stop in a sandy ditch. For entertainment's sake: second explosion.

"So, you know my basic story. Tell me about yours."

"Not much worth saying, really."

"If you're gonna lie, do so convincingly."

I try to figure out what makes a lie sound convincing, where my voice cracks or what visual clue I give out.

"Let me guess your story."

Laughs await – I'm sure of it. "Guess away." I lean back into the seatback some.

"Let's see. Your first girlfriend, your first 'true love', decided to end things at the end of the summer because she's going to a different college. And you needed to leave to show her how important you are to her. You left, didn't tell her, didn't tell her when you'd return, and so when you get back she'll see how important you are to her and she'll either try to make the long-distance thing work or she'll go to your college, which is inevitably worse than hers."

I think back over four years of high school. When I cover those all-to-fast fourteen-hundred days girls don't populate my memories. There's my freshman year when the dean of students tried to get me to sign a false statement about a fight I witnessed; there's Rick who became my best friend when I wouldn't lie against him. I see gym class and the bell at the top of the rope just inches away and my teacher, who bet with another teacher a week's lunches against me, shaking the rope to distract me, me yelling for him to stop that I'm going to fall, me falling twenty feet onto a pitiful map and lying for countless minutes waiting for the wind to come back; the teacher taking a very early retirement as a result of the law suit. There's Amy, lying on her bed in jeans and a tight sweater. She has been waiting for me for a while, my car had gotten a flat tire. Her parents had let me in, knowing me well. Amy was my first real girlfriend, but that didn't last more than a month before we decided things worked better when we kept each other at arm's length. I see Amy not letting me touch her arms or put my fingers up her sleeves. Amy slides out from Colander's passenger's seat and jogs to the Lake Michigan waterfront, just on the other side of the line where the sand gets darker. I follow her and she stands, facing me, with Lake Michigan backgrounding her in the half-light of early dusk, waves tapping a steady beat on the sand and rocks, seagulls squawking and flapping an accompaniment of sorts, a breeze coming off the lake and pushing the tips of her hair in front of her, the triangle of a large sailboat just millimeters from the line where sky kisses water. Amy leans forward and kisses me, wipes her lips with her index finger and puts it on my lips to stop me from saying anything. 'Don't talk. You'll spoil this,' she said, looking at the impressions her toes made in the sand. 'You're good at that – ruining moments.' She'd wanted to do that for months and, having done it, wouldn't ever again. 'Know that I don't think I can ever be as happy again as I just was,' she said. Amy said those types of things and when she did, no one ever rolled their eyes or found it melodramatic. She seemed to have a prescience of her life, a knowledge of how things would happen and that she couldn't stop it. A prescience I lack. An understanding that precludes my presence. I wasn't sure if she cried or not because of the rain; at least it rains in my memory. But she is the only girl I see in all four years.

"Not really."

"Oh. Well. Want to know a secret, something I've never told anyone before?"

Why do I get to hear it? "Sure."

"When I left, I left partly because I'd been dumped. But I got him back, you betchya. Here's what happened." She stops talking and listens, looks lost.

"You okay?"

"Yes, just listening to the music."

The radio is off. I check.

"Anyway, I found his diary. His 'journal.' He kept it in a box under his bed. It took some work, but I got into the box. He had filled it with all these bad things about me. He'd done it during an 'off' period, but had thought them nonetheless. Well, he was all that was keeping me in Ohio. When he got home from work, I confronted him. He yelled."

"Seems logical."

"Perhaps in retrospect, yes. But love, it's odd when you're in it. But he leaves, tells me to be gone in half an hour or he'd call the cops. I left alright. But I also took his toilet paper, toothpaste, trash cans, deodorant. Nothing of significant value, but all kinds of convenience things. I took all his condiments, too."

I bite my tongue to keep from laughing. She sees it and chuckles, incorrectly assumes I'd be laughing with her.

"Left Ohio the next day. Had no reason to stay, after all." And Watersharer is silent again, as if listening to something beyond my ability to hear. "Do you hear that music?" she asks.

I hear wind and tires and engine. "No."

"Listen to it. It's better than the radio, better than anything. Except Brahms, or a recording of a Stokowski-conducted Beethoven's Ninth. All you hear is noise. Listen to each part and then put them together. The engine. It's got a pattern. There's a whirr to it but then there's the ticking of the fan, the clicking of something loose underneath. There's a periodic 'whish' as something releases pressure. Then there's the tires and beyond that the clapping as the car moves over the lines of tar in the pavement." Watersharer honks the car horn. "The music needed that. Sometimes it's nice to contribute."

"It must get old."

"No, never. It's always different. Other cars add to the music. Big insects hitting the windshield add to the music. If I drive the same road over and over, I'll drive slowly sometimes to hear the music differently."

"Bet the other drivers love that."

"Not my concern. Besides, their honking adds to the music." Watersharer honks twice and looks at me again. "So you're out here because of love. Well, Merak, all I can say about love is this. If you're in it, you know. No one can tell you when you are or aren't. And unless you know how to let go of things, how to fully surrender yourself to a situation, you'll never know. I love music. I am in love with music. There is no greater love to have."

My Methodist upbringing hurls lines of scripture at me, tells me to use them, to explain what greater loves there are. I quiet the urge, surrender to my desire to be back at my car.

"That' all it is, Merak. You know or don't. So you go home and if you know you're in love with her, you tell her so and if she's in love with you, she'll know. This trip you took will prove it to her."

<«»>

When we get to my car she passes it a little and makes a U-turn. I open my door and take the bag of food and the gas can. The ashtray I set on the seat and already she has begun getting the trappings of travel from the backseat and re-placing them. Jessup rolls forward as she reaches in the back and her foot comes off the brake.

"Thank you so much, Watersharer, for going so far out of your way."
I hand her a twenty and she puts her palm up. "The Universe wants you to
have it." Watersharer looks at me, then the money, and decides that It does
want her to have it. "Before you go, can I take your picture?"

"I'm not really one for pictures. They're pretty intangible, you know.
Just images of something that's long gone."

"I'll always be able to remember who told me about the sweat lodges,
this way."

"Well, I reluctantly agree." Watersharer stands and walks to the front
of Jessup, resting her arm on the driver's side of his hood. She smiles widely,
teeth showing their cigarette stain, hair pushed left by the breeze, her legs
crossed at the ankles. I line her up vertically, Jessup on the left of the picture
– his grill seems almost to bend up at the sides – and take the photo.

"It'll turn out well, I'm sure. Before you go, have you ever heard of a
place called Antelope Canyon? I can't find it on any maps."

"Sure have. Got a map on ya?"

I hand her maps for each of the nearby states. "Alright, it's in
Arizona, in Page," she says, circling it on the map. "Lovely place."

"Thank you, Watersharer."

She gets back in her car and says to me, through the open windows,
"think about the sweat lodge, Merak. Find out who you are." She folds the
twenty and slides it into her sock, waves, and drives away.

My car, dusty and quiet, sits on the shoulder. I unscrew the gas cap
and pour the two gallons into my tank. When it empties I put the red ball in
my trunk. The towel on my cracked and taped seat is skin-reddeningly hot
but better than the vinyl would have been. I toss my shirt on the passenger's
side and open my sandwich. As I bite into the dry and salty ham, the sogified
tomato, I pump the gas pedal to prime the engine. When it starts, after a few
false alarms, the ratcheting feeling normal and safe, I lean back and exhale.
The radio, which predated presets and tunes with a sliding red bar behind

painted-on numbers, finds one station. In just three notes the music is clearly false happiness, the sort which populates the lyrics and repetitive chords of most modern songs. I think for a minute about how I know that, but stop, enjoying instead the knowing. I look at the dash, my hand on the column shifter. "What's your name?"

Colander does not reply; he never will – Colander is a good car, loyal and safe; he watches out for me but prefers a strictly business relationship. He is crotchety, too, like an angered old man forced into physical labor. I imagine him hitting me upside the head for asking such a stupid question. I make a U-turn and double back toward Page.

‹◊›

I arrive at a motel in Page, Arizona, and no one is in the office, no reading attendant, no sleeping concierge. The front door is propped open and a sign in the window says "vacancy." It flickers and moths fly around it inside and outside the office. The area behind the desk is messy. A phone, with black circles on the keypad, rests off the hook, buzzing loudly. I set it back on.

"Hello?"

No reply. The front door is the only way in or out of the office. On the counter a register book is open and in the past week shows that a man named "John Smith" rented out six or more rooms a night each night.

"Anyone around?" There is no bell, no button for service. I walk back to my car and sit, reading about the night sky in the dome lamp's light. After an hour I go back to the office. Still no one mans the desk. I walk behind it, leave forty dollars with a note to the manager stating I'd be in room 19 if he had questions, and take the key from a drawer under the phone.

I park at the end of the row, by a stairwell. For a while I fight with my trunk before it opens. "This problem would be so much less so if your backseat folded down." I stop and look at the ground between my legs. "This talking to you thing is going to stop." Everything inside my trunk is warm. I set my pillow and sleeping bag in a corner of it. I set my hands on the camera case, over the small lines of dust from Anna's hands, let the heat travel from the case into my palms, up my arms, through my back. I carry my camera, suit, and duffels upstairs to my room.

The shower runs on hot for ten minutes but still only cold water comes. I brush my teeth at the sink at the end of the room and look into the bathroom waiting for steam. After giving up on a warm shower, I stick just my head in; the water shrinks my scalp as I hold my hair in and turn the basin tannish-red. When it finally stops I dry my hair with a washcloth and walk into the hotel room. I haven't seen a bed in nearly two weeks. I put my pajamas on, sit on the edge of it, and lay backwards.

3
Apogee

The room would be aphotic, cave-black, except for a square frame of light intruding around the drapes. It ribbons across two walls, the sink and mirror at the back of the room, the ceiling, and the messed, crumpled sheets of my bed. I dry my hair with one of the hotel's white towels and wrap it around my waist. Shower steam, which only took minutes to arrive this time, has moved out of the bathroom and fogs the mirror's top margin. From under the line of steam I stare back at myself.

"Ready to take on another canyon?"

"Yes."

"Good."

I flip on the light and exhaust fan, which clicks in the ceiling like train wheels on tracks. My reflection seems like a strange photo, more like my father. Skinny as I am, he had been more so. A photo labeled "Lake San Cristobal 1972," from when he was a Boy Scout, showed his troop wearing swim trunks in front of a dock and tree with a tire swing and behind that a flat expanse of lake. On the end of the middle row stood my father, shoulders like assembled twigs, ribs like the strings of a harp, and legs built similar to high-tension towers.

Across my reflection's chest, rib lines show faintly. The shoulders are there, too. But it is not like looking at myself in the mirror, and it seems as if the desert has made me gaunt like my father. I flex in front of the mirror. To the reflection I pull punches. To the reflection I lunge forward. To the reflection I am intimidation made flesh. Only to the reflection.

"That's how I get psyched before work and big meetings, you know." My father stands behind my reflection.

"I did know that."

"Just making sure."

I sit on the counter, lengthwise, the towel hanging like Pharaoh's garb, my feet against the far side of the counter and wall. "Any specific reason you're here?"

"Just thought you may have questions you want to ask."

"Lots."

"Ask away."

"Why stay married?"

"Divorce doesn't happen in our neighborhood."

"Like how the Mitchells stayed married after the husband got caught with the babysitter?"

"Yeah, but I'm not consigned to a celibate life, nor do I have to buy tanzanite and platinum jewelry and a Mercedes each year just to keep living at home. That woman's a hardcore bitch." He looks at the wall, walks to the TV and runs his finger on it. "This is the shittiest motel ever."

"Yeah?" I turn my blistered foot sideways some. It has taken on the translucent pallor of the rest of my skin, to an extent, but is still heartily ruddified. Around the trimmed edges the skin is pressed flat. I still let it air at night and it won't be fully healed for weeks, but at least I will be able to walk on it without limping, for short distances.

"Yeah," he says, leaving.

From my duffel I take out tough, black, long-inseam jean shorts. I match them with an old, gray short-sleeve shirt that says 'I like pornography' above a smiley-face with an overly giddy, toothy grin and squinted eyes. Whenever I wore it to school I had to wear an overshirt so my parents didn't see it. Their conservative Methodist views wouldn't have allowed me outside with this shirt on. I ease the drapes open to see the sunrise over the desert. The view is blocked by a billboard calling me 'baby' and saying I've come a long way. Even here, in this mostly sterile place that seems as far as man will get from Earth, without leaving, there is, of all things, a billboard. Light, highlighted by sand and dust in the air, breaks past the ad on all sides; one side of the broken light comes through my window. The TV top is dusty; there is no finger line. I use my shower towel to wipe the dust off. "Shittiest motel ever."

I pull the curtains together and walk outside, careful to remember my key. The hotel could be ripped from any bad desert movie set. The doors are white and the building red-painted cinder block and the neon sign in the office that says vacancy in bright green still flickers from time to time, but without moths. The sign at the corner of the parking lot simply says "motel" and is adorned by mock railroad crossing gates, the lights of which flash as one.

In the light it looks bad, poor. Far worse than just ten hours ago when I pulled in – tired and sore from another day in the sun – at a different place, different state, than I had expected to be in that morning. Antelope Canyon is an excursion, a declension from the plan.

Rust seeps from inside the motel steps and under the red paint, the bright red, between brick- and fire engine-red, paint. Some of the spots are just stalactite-like cuspids, others trace cracks in the cement hidden by paint then drop suddenly downward.

The air smells broken, like the collected scents of a dozen collapsed trailers and a thousand cars-on-blocks have come to meet here. It almost makes me not want breakfast.

Next door is a hole-in-the-wall café and the smell of coffee and smokey bacon pulls me. Walls: vinyl siding. Roof: Sheet shingles. Sign: Bug carcass-filled plastic letters. Name: Sally's. Window: Monstrous with a frosted image of a gussied-up old woman.

Sally's is all griddle, fry vats and sandwich prep area on the right with a long counter and stools then tables and booths on the left. There are a few rugged, hatted, tired men sitting at the counter, and a woman, very similar to the smiling face on the window, but fatter and with a long wattle, who stands over the griddle, sucking on a straight pretzel and not smiling.

A half a tambourine on the door clicks as I open it and then again as the door slams shut, shaking the front window. I jump forward. No one in the diner flinches.

"Sorry, very sorry," I say.

"For?" asks the woman.

"The door."

"Have a seat." As she talks her wattle moves like someone trying to dance and failing.

I sit at the nearest stool

"What'll ya have?"

"Um, I dunno. Do you have menus?"

She sighs and bites into her pretzel. A piece breaks and lands on the grill surface, but she doesn't seem to notice. The grill has stacks of cooked bacon, sausage, and a pile of scrambled eggs on one side. "This griddle's your menu." She points with a blackened metal spatula. "We also got toast. How do you want your eggs?"

"Over easy, please."

"Two or three?"

"Three, please."

"Why, aren't you Mr. Manners. Bacon or sausage?"

"Bacon. And two slices wheat toast. Water to drink, please."

"See, now you got it. Coming right up."

Sally takes three eggs from a small hotel-room-style fridge next to the grill. She holds each egg in her hand like a knuckle ball, taps the shell on the edge of the grill, and pulls it open with one hand. The eggs fall an inch to the

64

surface and begin to whiten and seize. She takes two pieces of supermarket brand bread and puts them on the griddle, too. While they cook she fills a cup with ice, holds it under a tap, and sets it in front of me. The water is marginally cloudy. From under the counter she takes a fork, knife, spoon and napkin dispenser, setting them at my place.

"Oh geez," I say. "I forgot my wallet. Can I go grab it real quick? I'm in that hotel right there."

"I expect to get paid, so yeah, go grab it." Sally chuckles. Sally's wattle bounces.

The door slams shut, bringing me to a stop before I run across the street and up the rusting concrete steps to my room. I unlock it, get my wallet, leave, lock it, run back to the restaurant, walk in and hold the door as it shuts. At my seat is a plate with three over-easy eggs, five slices of bacon, and two pieces of toast. Next to it is a caddy with room-temperature packets of strawberry jelly. I break the yolks of my eggs and dab up the spreading yellow with the toast. The bacon is alternately soggy and crunchy. The water tastes like sulfur.

From the end of the bar someone says "hey, kid. You in the jeans and the gray shirt."

I turn. "Me?"

"You the only kid in here?" He looks around. "Yup. So I must be talkin' to you."

"Oh, yeah. I'm sorry about the door."

"Ain't that. I see you like pornography." His head is scarred from something, and the scarring goes down onto the left of his face. He has no eyebrow, no left muttonchop to twin the right side, and his mustache ends early, too. The scars have their own topography, canyons and valleys forming a series of progressing, southward "V"s, but I don't stare.

"Ron, don't harass my customers."

Ron looks at her and speaks. "I ain't harassin' no one, Sally. This is business." The left of his lips don't move. "I got some porn I sell outta my trailer," he says to me.

"No one wants to buy your bootleg pornos, Ron."

"Sally, please, I'm discussin' a transaction with my new buddy here. Anyway, it's some crazy shit. Shit you can't buy in the stores. I'll sell it cheap, because I like the looks of you."

"Ah, no thanks. I actually don't like pornography." The lie, about not liking porn, falters across my tongue because navigating lies of commission is, to me, like knowing only the destination and not the directions.

"No one doesn't like porno. Even Sally here likes porno."

"First you want me out of this, then you want me in it. Make up your mind, Ron."

"Anyway, it's good stuff. Women putting two of everything everywhere."

"Thanks, but no thanks. I'm just not interested today."

"What about bein' in one? Ever thought of that? I employ some honey chicks and you can do whatever wherever to 'em. Only pays like a hundred bucks, but you get to spend a day bangin' my sweet, sweet wahinis."

That may be the creepiest thing I have ever heard. "Er, maybe next time."

"Whatever, jack."

When I finish, Sally puts the check in front of me. It says "3.50. Sorry about Ron. Sally."

I leave a five dollar bill on top of the check, wave and thank her for the great meal, and leave, holding the door as it shuts behind me. A man in tight jeans, a black shirt, and a wide-brimmed Stetson hat passes me. He opens the door and yells "Hey, Sally!"

"Mornin', Hector."

The door slams shut behind him. I jump but no one inside even notices. At the stairs up to the motel's second floor I look at the concrete steps and wonder how they rust. And how they rust in the desert. In my room is my luggage and camera. I check to make sure I have everything, including checking under the bed. Grandfather once said that I should always take the Gideons' Bible from a hotel because whoever used the room after me surely wouldn't need it. I open the night stand drawer to take the Bible, but it's already been nicked – the phonebook, too. I leave a five dollar tip on the counter next to the sink.

The sun is higher now, the air warms but is kept in check by a gentle, sandy breeze.

The front office is still empty. My money sits on the desk, under the note, just like I left it. I look around for a camera, wipe the key clean of finger prints in my shirt hem and hang it back on the key rack, sure not to get more fingerprints on it. My money I put back in my wallet. I look back at the desk.

"Don't steal," says my father, leaning against the doorframe.

"It's not stealing. It's a refund for bad customer service."

"What goes around has a way of coming back around, so goes the adage"

I press my hands to my ears and shake my head. Am I going crazy? I don't know. It all would have happened, had to happen; if this trauma had not happened then another would have, or one would have been made-up. Like my father who ran, and my grandfather who stayed when his family left, I, too, had to take my future in my hands and try to change it. My father's voice is just my own internal monologue taking on the role of my conscience. Nothing more.

‹◊›

Antelope Canyon is a sandstone slit in the ground created by water washing the sandstone away a grain at a time. It is an unintrusive stretch outward surrounded by the reddest sand I have ever seen. I bend down on the path to it and take an empty film canister out of my pocket and fill it.

At the entrance is a small covered table with a cooler stashed underneath. Disposable bathroom cups of water sell for fifty cents each. There is also an entrance fee. I pay it. An L.A. Times on the table is folded back to the stocks section. The date at the top is August 11th. "Is it really the eleventh?"

The man who takes my money is Indian. "Yes." His hair is short, buzzed to within an inch of his head, but thick like zoysia or Saint Augustine. "This is the rainy season," he says. "This canyon is prone to flash floods. If you hear a sound like a stampede, or a train, do not try to climb out of the canyon – you will not make it. Press your back to the nearest wall and hold your breath when the water hits you. It is your only chance."

"Do floods happen often?"

"Normally, we keep up on the weather. Flood water drains down this ditch," he points to a ditch running to the slit. "No weather warnings today, but sometimes we are caught off-guard." He shrugs. "Don't worry, it's too early for the rain to have started, really." He points at his watch. "Normally, the rain is an afternoon thing, when the cumulus clouds," said pointing to the sky and slowly forming puffs, "made from the sun evaporating water all day," he swirls his finger at the ground in tight circles, "reach capacity and rain. We warn everyone, just in case."

"Okay." I nod and thank him. Maybe he thought that because I am a kid I don't understand evaporation. Or maybe because of my dress and my questions and my obvious out-of-stateness he felt the need to explain the evaporation cycle as if I were in second grade. He takes money from someone else. My camera and wide-angle lens, simply because it is the most versatile, hang around my neck. I slide down the sandstone of the entrance, feeling sand come off of it and paste in the sweat behind my knees. Just before my head goes below ground I look to my left and near the edge of the canyon is a single flower. Around it is sand too hot to touch but there is a single yellow bud on a pale green stalk feet from the nearest plant.

It is not a dark canyon – in fact it is bright. The walls of the canyon are steep and tall, it may look similar to what the Red Sea was like when it parted. The sandstone is orange, not as red as the desert. The rock moves like water, supine and soft in its curves and waves, lithesome and svelte with its turns and drops: a lithological Terpsichore.

The path is about a foot's-width across in places, punctuated by steep declinations of a few feet and ripples of stone. I put one knee to the ground next to my foot and press my hand on a particularly large wave then mirror it with my right. I walk my hands forward, keeping my foot and knee planted. My camera swings from my neck in an oval of strap. I lean forward and pull my legs up so all my weight is on my hands, set my feet down and walk onward; my limp begins.

At occasional wide spots I pass groups, then later they pass me. We all take our time on the descent, take photographs, too bewitched to converse with each other. In large, round, flat areas there are small pits where pebbles have gotten trapped and spun there by water, digging faster. There is water in the pits and in depressions along the path.

I descend and work my body; the blister pulses a cadence; sweat pops into beads and falls to the fluid floor. At a steep downslope, climbers press their feet onto one side and their shoulders to the other then slowly step and scoot. Hikers stop and begin their walk home. Even with strobes of growing pain up my leg and jogging my back, I make the scoot down because I feel that at no other time in my life will I ever be back here.

At a narrow point I stop to take photos. Pictures of a deep pit off to the left, of a looped outcropping in front of me, and the steep wedge downward. Behind me someone clears their throat. It is a short, pale kid. His face is round, hair like a copper scrub pad. Around the waist he is a little chubby but his elbows skeletal; his face and shoulders are a bas relief of angles. I apologize, cover my camera lens, and sit on the rock slope, feet outstretched. I pull myself towards my feet, push them out, and do that four more times until I reach the bottom. The kid behind me walks down the embankment with no problem and turns to face me.

"You didn't have to move on," he says. "I just needed to get past."

"S'okay, I need to keep moving. Stopping is what's hard."

He shrugs, says 'true that,' and keeps walking, placing his feet to the best places, focusing his eyes high above him at the narrow line of daylight angling into the canyon.

In time I reach the end of the hike-able canyon. At the end is a deep, black pit with a two-by-four stuck some feet down it. The pale kid crouches on the balls of bare feet over the pit. His shirt is tied around his waist and most of it rests on the sandstone.

"Can I take your picture?" I ask. "This would be a great shot."

The wall behind him is the merging of rip currents fixed in sandstone. Water would come to this point in the canyon, move over where he sits and then whorl down the hole with the two-by-four. He rolls his head backward, counterclockwise, his neck sounding a loud pop. He bounces lightly on his feet and re-does his crouch, making it more even, making his balance more precise. The kid looks at the camera; every muscle in his face limpens. Though the picture will, I hope, be one of pure indifference, he has put a lot of care into making it look that way. I raise the camera and take the picture.

"Took you a while to focus."

"I always bring it out of focus then put it back once, for good luck and to make sure I get the focus right."

"That's a nice camera," he says in a voice as close to flute music as a human voice can be.

"Thank you. I saved for a long time for it."

"You a pro?"

I walk to the canyon across from him, here there is a comfortable three feet of space occupied by a massive hole between us. "I used to want to be. Ever heard of a guy named Reichert? German guy. Does landscapes and cityscapes."

"I don't know much about picture taking."

"Well, Reichert was giving a lecture at the Art Institute of Chicago. I had a buddy of mine forge me a student ID and I got in to see him. During the lecture he talked about how hard it was to get where he was and still how few great photographers ever make back the money they put into their work. This guy's at the top of his game and if he were to have a bad year, it could sink him. That's when I decided to just keep this a hobby."

"Makes sense," he says, turning to look down the canyon. "Sometimes I wonder what's down there."

"Looks dark."

"I know. Once I grabbed a rock along the path, about the size of a urinal puck, and dropped it down. It hit something then splashed."

"You come here often, then?"

"Once or twice a week. I live nearby. This place is nicer than home. My name's Michael."

"Merak."

"Merak. Merak. Now that's a name I've never heard. Sounds . . . Slavic?"

"I think it's actually Arabic, but my parents thought it was Italian."

For a while Michael and I look down the pit, at the board. He tries to reach it with his feet, to knock it loose and send it into the pit, but is inches too short. I set my camera down then hold myself above the hole with my arms, my right foot on the edge, and lower my left foot to the lumber. I hook it and lift, the board doesn't want to move, but with an extra hard pull it does, moving up, giving way, and pulling me down as it goes. I fall but grab the base of the hole, at the path floor, with my arms. The board lets go then clunks off rock before splashing.

"Help," I say, trying to yell it but I hear only the sound of an old door.

There is no rock below or behind my legs, which kick and feel, hoping for rock, surprised by its absence. Michael drops and grabs my wrists. He puts his feet against the canyon wall and extends his legs, pulling me back over the edge and onto the loose till of the path. He sits on the path and I lie on it for a second with most of my legs still hanging into the pit.

"Thanks, man," I say.

Michael smacks my shoulder when we've stood. "No prob, bro. You'd have done the same for me."

"True that. True that."

I wipe at my eyes with the backs of my hands, trying to make it look like I've got dust in them. While I kicked my feet backward, like a blind man expecting a step which doesn't exist, I realized that I haven't talked to my parents in twelve days. I see them in the house, sitting at the dining room table, the eight-foot by five-foot solid, foggy glass supported by four pine columns coated to look like blackened cement, talking to a city policeman who gives them the details of where I was and how I died. He would set my camera and rolls of film along with my travel journal on the table for them and in time they would develop the photos and try to piece together my trip. Mother will sit with a seat or more separating Father. Mother will slowly page through photos and wonder who Anna is. Father will read the journal. 'You're free to leave me for Brian, now.'

They wish they could tell me things – what things are a mystery – but all the years' worth of advice my father would want to give. Things I had heard him say on the phone to coworkers like 'don't get too drunk at your reception – you'll have wifely duties, you know,' then laughing. Or my mother with 'the diaper gets folded left flap then right and the safety pin goes here, like this' and me saying 'disposables – duh'

But more, the conversation I'd never have had hits; like a fist – a very, very big fist – there comes an awareness that I'm going to have to explain all this at some point. The note was not enough. I sit next to the hole. It's not so scary, now, compared to the idea of a conversation with us having too much to say to each other.

"Phew, that woulda been bad." Michael looks down the hole and then back at me, raising his eyebrows.

"I'd have been fine." This is me trying to make the whole thing look meaningless.

Michael sits opposite me, sweat is crowned jewels on his forehead. "At least there's water down there. May have broken your fall."

"Yeah," I say slowly. "No telling how stagnant or skunky it is."

"Or what kind of disease lives in it."

"Yeah. Bad news all around."

"By chance, did you count how many seconds it took for that length of two-by to hit water?"

"Ah, no. I was busy trying not to see how many seconds it'd take me to hit water."

"Good point. But too bad, we coulda calculated the distance."

"Next time." Perhaps it is clear that that question is a vagrant here.

"Next time."

As if there is a hole between us, we look at each other in quick glances and then around at the cavern.

"I said before how I don't know much about picture taking, right?" Michael must need to fill the hole with words. "Well, here's why. There's this picture at my place of my mom, dad and I. It was a photo taken for the police department, all the officers were photographed with their families. But it's not true, you know? The photo, that is. Photos lie. They don't reflect how things are." These words, however, don't fill but instead tunnel.

I pause before replaying, the sudden openness worrisome; perhaps he wants something I may or may not be willing to give. "So I've heard. Why are you telling me this?"

"What else are we gonna talk about? I'd rather not keep thinking about that near miss. Take a picture of some section of rock."

I find an interesting one and I do.

Michael walks to it and rubs his hands all over it. Sand falls from it. "Your photo's now a lie. That piece of wall is different now. If you took a second photo of it they may look identical, but there's a difference."

"But the picture shows how it was then. It tells the truth about its appearance for that sixtieth of a second."

"But life, it changes – the photo doesn't."

"I still don't get your beef with it. Yeah, life changes, it's like that, but photos serve to remind us of how things once were, to bring up happier times and jog the memories our mind has filed away in rarely-used storage. They show us where we once were, what we've lost or what we've gained. In ten years I'll still remember you because your photo will be in my collection somewhere."

"But that won't be me. In ten years I may be dead, or may be fat and bloated working security at the asylum."

"Then memory is a lie, too."

Michael looks up and left, watches a line of sunlight on the wall. "I suppose so." We look at each other and the hole, then at the path up. "How about we get out of here," he says. "Oh, hey, can you give me a ride home? It's only about two miles but it's hot to be walking it."

Ah, yes. Indeed, it's something I'd have been willing to give. The openness wasn't needed. Perhaps knowing that would not have changed his manner of asking, though. "Sure thing, man. I don't have A/C, though."

"A/C?"

"Air conditioning."

"Oh, yeah."

My watch says it is 12:10. The drive will be hot.

‹‹›

The walk, while only two miles, is deceptive. The drive is closer to ten. The air coming off the desert now that the sun is vertical and uncloudblocked is baking temperature. My arm, out the window, feels it. My hand, working its fingers in the passing air, feels it. My legs and back, pressed against the towel on the seat, feel it. Michael also feels it, but deals better than I do. He sweats less, and even seems to enjoy the hot cocoon.

Within a few minutes on the rural highways going away from the canyon and toward Michael's home, the temperature needle on my car has begun to rise. I turn the heat on full, blowing engine air up the windshield and across the roof of the car. Michael suggests I slow down and I do.

Sand and gravel crunch under Colander's mismatched tires and the blowing heat from the dash sounds like whimpers and screams, alternately. But they're not. Though my car has a name, of sorts, and I talk to it, and often its noises sound very human, it is just a piece of machinery and the sum of it is just the sum of its parts, or so I will tell myself if he breaks.

"How far are we?" I ask.

"About a mile and a half. Can your car make it?"

"I hope so." But Colander cannot make it. Half a mile or so down the road he overheats and rolls to motionlessness, half on the shoulder and leaning gently toward a roadside gully.

"Damn," I say.

"I saw you limping back at the canyon. You gonna be okay to walk?"

"If need be, yeah. But I need to let this guy cool down." I pop the hood.

Michael and I look at it, into the empty coolant reservoir. "I got some water you can have back at my place. No coolant, though, sorry."

"Water's cool, I'll just get coolant at the next filling station."

We walk toward his home. "Better it happen here than where there is no one." Michael stops and takes off his shirt, again, tying it around his waist. He then takes off his shoes and walks barefoot in the sand.

"I ran outta gas the other day where there is no one. Got a ride, but it wasn't much better than hiking through the desert, honestly."

"I hear ya. Some nutjobs out here. The desert, it either hones your perceptions, clarifies the world to you, or it just makes you lose it."

"I imagine so . . . don't your feet burn?" I say, taking off my shirt as we walk.

"You get used to it. I like the heat, the burning, how it wraps itself around you and says 'you are mine,' and is afraid to let go under penalty of death. It won't scar or anything, but it releases endorphins."

"Endorphins?"

"Chemicals in the brain and gut. Natural – endogenous – morphines. When you feel pain it releases them to make you feel less pain. It's pleasing, a natural drug of sorts."

"Okay."

"Try it. If you don't want to take your shoes off then just touch the sand here with your hand."

I bend over and put a hand on the sand. I feel it burn for a second or two then, suddenly, like a warm, halcyon wave – cascading through my body as if water through a canyon – endorphins soften the pain and loosen muscles. I smile at Michael. "I like that." When I lift my hand the imprint remains just beyond the shadow of a tall prickly pear cactus. I pick up a handful of sand and sift it through my fingers, trailing it as I walk. "Have you lived out here your whole life?"

"No. My mom died seven years ago. We lived in California until then. This nice little development. My dad was a police officer. A detective. I remember it being a good place, happy. But I was a kid, who knows if that's really how it was."

Michael's voice is less musical when his mother comes up. The tones, sounds, become asyndetic, staccato. His feet leave skids in the sand.

"Anyway, we lived in this subdivision, a quiet, blue-collar place. Most of the people living there were cops, firemen, construction workers, salt-of-the-earth and what not. But every house had both parents working. It wasn't a cheap neighborhood. The houses were brick or ashlar, the driveways concrete. There were front lawns with a high palm tree in each. At the end of the block was this Presbyterian church. We went there. You Presby?"

"Methodist. Big church, one of those ones where you get the gift of anonymity, even from the reverend."

"Our's was huge, too. Congregation over two-thousand. Dr. Roberts, the pastor, still knew every congregant's first name, though. The first floor was brick, the original church, the old wing they called it, but the rest of it, the second and third floors, the chapels, the steeple – more a steep triangle than traditional steeple – were all white. So white. You should have seen them in the sun. They just, they, I don't know."

"Luminesced?"

"Luminesced. Luminesced. I like that. Yes, that's what the walls did. And in the dawn the building was blue and at dusk it was red and orange. Then at night they had these spotlights on it, three, and they have these thick black plastic things on so that three crosses shone on the broadest side of the building. I could see them from my bedroom window."

"Musta been a bit creepy."

77

"Only when I would bring my dad's Playboys back to my room to look at, or steal one of his beers.

"Then my mom died. She was in the wrong place at the wrong time, getting some sandwiches from a deli for the family on her way home from work and the store was held up. They found her, the employees and other customers in back, in the cooler, everyone shot execution-style with a sawed-off twelve-gauge shotgun. Dad worked on the case, not officially. He worked on it at home, at lunch, all night.

"He took to speed, first. Needed it to stay awake at work because he wasn't sleeping. He'd steal it out of the evidence locker. Small bits first, enough not to be noticed. Then it got more and he stole coke and heroin, too. Snorted it, shot it, whatever he could do. Everyone knew. They tried to help but he pushed them all away and, in the end, was kicked off the force. For good reason, too. Sooner or later he would have killed a suspect or driven into a school bus or something. They gave him a lot of slack, hoped he'd pull it together."

"That sucks. Your parents loved each other a lot?"

"Yeah. Mushiness abounded. Anyway, he hasn't ever fully cleaned up, blew most of the life insurance money, too, was jobless for years, and now we're here. He bought this plot of land dirt cheap. Only thing was no one told him the well was polluted and he didn't do anything about it until it was too late. The court dismissed his case to reverse the contract because he waited too long."

I stumble over the picked-clean skull of a large lizard. "I've been kinda pondering your view of photos. At your mom's funeral, I bet the minister said that as long as people remember her, she'll live on."

"Yeah, standard funeral stuff."

"So, see, she lives in your memories, in your photos. These things aren't harbingers of a dead, removed time, they're the preservers of a moment of life. Photos keep things alive for us."

"I'm not convinced, but I'll think about it. What if something is never photographed?"

"By choice or happenstance?"

"Let's say choice."

"Then there's a conscious choice on someone's part to allow that thing to be left to the forgotten parts of history," I say

"That's sad."

"In a way, perhaps."

"Anyway, enough philosophy. What brings you out here?"

I tell him, point-of-fact style.

"Damn. Still got it better than me."

"Yes, I do."

We walk for a while not talking, kicking cans and bolts and stones along the roadside. I am taking in what he has told me and trying to build a mental image of his family.

At interesting clouds, Michael points. Big enough ones rest on dark, slanting columns of rain, about to tip over sending the cloud to the ground. Around us are large saguaro and prickly pear cacti, some with pieces eaten away. Some flower with red or yellow buds. One particularly large saguaro cactus has a hole where birds chirp.

Michael's home is a silver/blue Airstream, resting on a structure of six-by-sixes. The two rear axles are tireless and rusted. The back roof is dented some. I had not expected anything as bad, and there is nothing to be done to hide the deep inhale and upright stance I take. He notices and frowns, slightly, but nods. The stairs to the front door are broken and one step threatens to sluff off when I put my foot on it.

"Wait here," says Michael. "I need to make sure my old man is passed out. He doesn't like me going to the canyon, so I have to sneak out and in while he's asleep. He's also paranoid. I don't know if it's from the drugs or what, but no one's allowed in the house except me and him. He sleeps with a gun on his night stand, just in case." He opens the trailer door and walks in.

The windows around the trailer are open, but the blinds are closed. The rear of the Airstream is dented in more places than just the large one visible from the road, and the red plastic taillight covers are broken, the shards under the axles. In the driveway is an old Indian motorcycle. It is dull, windblown, patched with small dabs of body replacer. The leather of the seat is pallid but not torn. Michael opens the door and signals for me to come inside.

"He's asleep. Works midnight security at a nearby asylum for Indians and poor whites. It's a bad place. I hear him tell stories about doctors doing unauthorized tests on patients. I didn't used to believe them until I worked there for a summer."

The Airstream is hot and smells like rotting meat, a smell I know from the summer the convenience store's cooler broke and all the food in it warmed and began to spoil in the two shifts before I got in to deal with the problem. Rotting meat is one of those smells that gets in your hair and clothes, like smoke, and takes days and multiple washings to remove. Rot is also the kind of smell that is never forgotten and even now, two years later, the smell carries with it the ten-hour day I spent in the cooler with my manager removing the meat and scrubbing every surface with bleach.

The counter is immaculate except for a pile of dirty dishes in the sink and a large plate of chicken pieces, mostly bones and tendons, dried, loitered on by a swarm of tiny flies. A dog lies on the floor. At one time it may have been a retriever, but now it is a sad, sad mongrel with patches of missing hair, scars like gopher tunnels across bare sections of skin, and ringworm. It looks up at me, sighs, and rolls over. The other side is worse: less hair, more scarring, pits in the skin which seep a yellow mash. Michael takes me back to his room. "The trailer's not hooked up to water or plumbing, so don't bother with the sink." He takes a gallon jug of water from under his bed and hands it to me. To the left and front are windows, open with the blinds cracked. This room is the only one that does not smell of rot. In fact, the air is somewhat breathable. The carpet is old and ruined and the dust of disintegrating padding comes through it, but compared to the other rooms, Michael's bedroom air is cleanliness made manifest. To the right is a closet with slatted switchblade doors. On the bottom of one of the doors are three missing slats.

In the kitchen the refrigerator door opens. "Mike, you eat the last of the ham?"

Michael looks at me, his eyes wide. He points at the closet.

Carrying the water, I open the switchblade doors and climb in. It's mostly empty except for a pile of dirty clothes that stink of sweat. The smell in the closet is harsh and my head throbs in it. Michael pulls the door shut as his father walks in.

"You eat the ham?"

Michael faces his father who just now walks in view. He is tall, fat with no shirt and a back papered in thick, curly black hair scaling his shoulders and down his upper arms. The hair on his head is matted and pushed off to the side. Along his belt line is a small pistol in a policeman's holster. His pants are part of a security guard's uniform.

"I did. I gave some to the dog. He was hungry."

"He's dying, you know. Slowly, like we all do, ultimately. Oh, Mike." The man grabs Michael in his arms and hugs him closely, pulling his face close into his shoulder. Michael hugs back, his hands on his father's shoulder blades, fingers tight to keep the hair from touching the insides. "Don't you ever die, you got it? Not until after I do. I couldn't lose you, too." He lets go of Michael and walks out of the room.

From the kitchen walks the sound of a bone being broken open and Michael's father sucking the marrow from it. I almost vomit in disgust. The marrow was old, could be infested or rancid. He drops it on the floor and says "I hope it breaks apart in your throat and ends your suffering." The dog's teeth click on the bone.

Michael stands. In the kitchen I hear the sound of pots clanking, the bone breaking. A steel pad scrubs the inside of a pan, circling, sounding like a parent shushing a toddler. The refrigerator opens and there is rustling. An egg is cracked open, fries. There is chopping.

Michael walks into the kitchen. I leave the closet to get fresh air, and sit next to his door frame.

"What did you do today, son?" the father scrambles the egg with a fork.

"Went to the canyon."

"I told you I don't want you doing that."

"It's safe in the morning."

"Someday that canyon's gonna flood and there'll be people in there. I don't want you to be one of those people. At least don't go in the rainy season."

"I was looking forward to going back tomorrow."

"What draws you to it, anyway?" He scrapes the egg onto a plate, turns off the stove.

"I dunno. You should go."

"I thought maybe it reminded you of your mother. She liked that sort of stuff, caves and canyons, beaches and forests. Very nature-oriented."

"I remember."

"I worry you'll forget her. You were young when she died."

"I won't."

"Have some eggs"

They have breakfast for lunch and talk. The smell of the food is standard, but stirs life in my stomach, which growls and threatens to reveal me.

I lean against the wall, feet to my butt, knees near my chest, and look at the water.

"Well, Merak, I bet you're glad I'm not like that. That's an unhealthy type of love."

I nod to my father who sits on the floor opposite me.

"Ah, but I know what you want to say. 'There's an unhealthy opposite, too.' There is. How many times do I have to tell you that your mother and I love you?"

I look at him.

"What do you want me to say? You call me out here and seem to want some kind of profound revelation, some sentence, phrase, or word that makes everything right. Your intent is admirable.

"When I was your age I left New Mexico for Chicago. For an architecture program. My father decided to stay behind in New Mexico when the rest of his family left. Both of these things happened after we found out what you just found out this past July.

"What you want to say is that pops stayed back for a girl, I left for school, and you're here for yourself. But that's losing the forest to see a single tree. You're not going to find out anything you don't already know."

Would my father really say that? No. No, I doubt he would.

"You want to say that grandfather stayed back for a girl, I left for school, and you're here for yourself. But that's losing the forest for a single tree. What more do you need to know? You're not making your own trail, no matter what you may think. Others have walked it before you. That's why it's a trail." Father stands, walks from the bedroom, to the kitchen.

In time Michael and his father finish and do the dishes, talking and laughing, they bump shoulders with jokes, freely act their conversation with their hands, or so their talk makes it seem. In time the father says he is going to clean up and Michael fetches two gallons of water from under his bed, acknowledging me with a nod.

"Put the dog outside, Mike." The door opens and Michael urges the dog outside.

"Good boy," he says, then the door shuts.

After another minute: "My old man's in the tub. It sucks, having to sponge bathe each day, but anyway, get going, Merak. And take care."

I walk outside and the door closes gently behind me. The dog lies on the ground in front of me. He bleeds from his mouth and is breathing shallowly, quickly. I look down at it. It is the saddest animal I have ever seen. Not because of the red loops on its side, or the gopher trails, but because it looks at me with fear and longing. It is afraid to die but wants the pain to end. I bend down to its mouth and break open the seal on the gallon of water. I pour a little, a capful at a time, into its mouth.

Mike is lucky, despite the trailer and the lack of running water. He will never doubt how his father feels for him nor how his mother felt. He has a whole other set of questions to ask and, in time, answer. His set has different problems, different enigmas, but it seems more appealing in a way than mine does.

I cap the water and begin the walk to my car, shirt tied around my waist, shoes and socks in my free fingers. Gravel and sand and cactus thorns stick to the soles of my feet. They feel like tiny branding irons but in a few seconds I am smiling, swimming in endorphin gaiety.

To the right, the wide-open right filled with sand and shrubs and desert water, even beyond that, is home. Home, a word with meaning far greater than the sum of its letters. Home is Chicago, the buildings behind the blue of Lake Michigan, Lake Shore Drive and Navy Pier, Wrigley Field.

Home is Deer Lake and my parents' house there, tucked between the neighbors with the matching BMWs and the neighbors who coordinate the block's holiday decorations. Home is a bedroom with prints of famous photographs taped to the walls. Home is my parents and, because of the near fall today, I realize they have been, are, and will be more important to me than I understood when I left Chicago twelve days ago.

Home is suddenly appealing and I can be there inside a week.

4
Sun Dream

Trips are like the path of a boomerang: the person, the boomerang, goes out and comes back. This boomerang, having passed his apogee, has begun his return, and heads to Interstate 70. Father must learn why I left, must be told, and must be made to understand that it is his fault I left. I will tell him all the things I have wanted to say but was not brave enough to at the first opportunity. But, for now, this is still Utah, not too far from Arizona, and I expect to have four or five more days to decide exactly what to say.

On a dirt road alongside this Utah highway is an old garage. The roof is shanty-style planks and inside are fossilized pieces of various old tractors. But night came hours ago and there are no hotels; this is abandoned so it seems as good a place as any to sleep. I do my nightly routine and sit under the stars listening to crickets and bats and stare at the sky, this wholly light pollution-free sky, stare at the moon's curl and wonder what it would be like to walk or drive on it, far as man has ever traveled from home.

And then I am in my father's garage working on his Ferrari, tightening some nuts near a belt. "That's not going to fix it," someone says, his voice and octave higher than the one coming from me.

"This will do it. I know it."

"It won't even start. New belts are like putting stitches in untouched skin when there's a huge gash just inches away."

"This'll work. It needs these anyway." What I want to say is 'I need this . . . toiling. Leave me be.'

And there is a sharp pain in my leg. The sun rises, a red orb in the distance bottomed by horizon lines. A short, shadow-cast figure holding a shotgun stands in front of it.

"Ain't no free sleep here, boy. Where you see a sign says 'Free Sleep Here'?"

"I, uh, am I awake?"

"Unfortunately for you, yes."

"I didn't know anyone owned this place. It looks abandoned."

"Maybe it is, maybe it ain't, but it's mine. You got till I count ten to be in your car or I start shootin'."

"What?"

"One."

Apologies flow while he counts. I slide out of my sleeping bag and grab it, my journal and pencil and have them in my backseat and my car started by 'seven.' I drive around the man's brand new super-duty pickup and onto the highway, bed hair not moving in the wind, me expecting to go back to the Ferrari any second.

My chest tightens, gut, too. The man sets his shotgun in the truck bed and watches me leave. I should not have slept there; I trespassed.

After some miles I stop at a twenty-four hour diner, order breakfast, shave and wash my hair in their sink with the orange liquid soap that smells of over-ripe mandarin oranges.

‹◊›

Along the side of the road, among the sand and scrub of the desert, is a silo. The side holds a billboard that says "Authentic Indian Vision Quests every Monday and Thursday at 8, 9, and 11 am. Next right, follow the signs."

"Why is there a silo in the desert?" I sigh and look at the ceiling and the black felt by the windshield which has started falling down in the last day. "Why am I still talking to you?"

I count off the days since the last time I knew the day of the week. It's Monday and I can make the nine o'clock quest easily. "Watersharer would be proud," I say and tap the steering wheel in time with the music.

The exit is a pale concrete road lined by expanses of bushes and occasional Joshua trees. The signs are small, single-post with boards nailed to them, painted and lettered. The individual planks are somewhat warped and none of the edges line. Some have popped remains of colored balloons hanging off them, twisting and swinging back and forth in the wind. The signs say "Your vision is 1000 yards ahead," "Your vision is 500 yards ahead," and "Your vision is the next left." The parking lot is well-rutted sand with spaced rocks for the border. I pull into a spot between two station wagons. There are maybe twenty cars in the parking lot, all said. The lot is ringed by Juniper and Joshua trees, the parking spots spotted with small evergreen weeds. At an end of the parking lot is a large adobe dome with about thirty people gathered outside. It is ten of nine.

Inside I am greeted by two tall, thin, long-haired white men. Their ears are pierced multiple times and feathers hang from them. Around their necks are necklaces of turquoise and wood beads strung on hemp rope.

"I am Squall Line," says one, holding his hand upright toward me. "This is Mule Deer Fights. Welcome to your vision. Would you prefer the nine or eleven o'clock?"

"Nine, please." I blink at them. It feels like I am in a vision or dream right now and that in no way can it end well.

"That's one-hundred and fifty dollars. Cash, check, or credit?"

I hand the man three fifty-dollar bills. What remains after: three-hundred and nineteen dollars.

"Mule Deer Fights will be your guide today, please take this," says Squall Line, handing me a small pamphlet, "read it and set it in the basket by the door outside.

The pamphlet says each vision quest is divided into ten people (there is a graphic of two rows of five bathroom sign-style people) including the guide (one of the people is red.) No one brings food, not even snacks, or water, illustrated by red circles with prohibitive slashes; one has a bottle, one a picture of a hamburger, and one a picture of a candy bar. The quest is an all-day event and leaves at eight (crossed out by hand), nine, or eleven AM exact (shown by a clock face with the big hand on the twelve and a little hand on the nine and one on the eleven) and will return around ten PM (the big hand is on the ten and the little on the twelve.) I set the pamphlet, which is fraying along the fold lines, in the basket and leave the small hut with Mule Deer Fights.

Outside, I join the group of about thirty people. Mule Deer Fights calls for our attention then he and Squall Line whoop for a while – calling spirits, they say when they finish.

"Most of you have met me, I am Mule Deer Fights. I was given this name on a vision quest, much like you are about to take."

A man with jeans, a palm leaf print shirt and straw hat whispers to me 'why are the guides white?' I shrug.

"Those of you assigned to me, please group over here on the left. Those of you going with Squall Line please go to the middle and if you're with Sun Dream go to the right."

Squall Line and Mule Deer Fights go to their side and from the group a thin, short, dark-red-haired girl with gentle features emerges to stand in the middle. The man who asked me about the guides' whiteness moves to Sun Dream's group. I walk up to him.

"You're here, too?"

"No, I'm with Mule Deer, but can we trade?"

He looks at me, then at Sun Dream, back at me and understanding crosses his face. "Sure thing."

"Thanks, man. I owe ya."

89

Sun Dream's voice is loud, despite her diminutive stature. She is maybe five feet even, almost a foot shorter than me. "If you have food or water, leave them here. Our staff will store them for you in a refrigerator. You will all take part of the sweat lodges with you." She is pretty, even though her hair is short. "We will pick those up at the forest line."

The other people in my group are older than I. Most look to be in their forties, one couple may be in their seventies. They wear polo shirts and khaki shorts. I have on hiking shoes, shorts, and a pale blue shirt with a white caricature of a hand making the 'okay' loop-and-extended-fingers. Today will be hot – today already is hot.

When we leave the immediate vicinity of the hut, the juniper trees end and the area returns to desert. Through the shrubs and cacti and Joshua trees a path is beaten in sneaker treads. Sun Dream has with her a long walking stick and explains it is for shooing rattlesnakes off the path. "If you hear a rattling," she says, "stop and yell for your guide. We're trained in moving them safely. Don't touch them, move toward them, or panic if you see one we miss. That said, we won't miss any. We may not even see them. It's been a light year for snakes." She explains that the heavier than usual rains have given rise to plenty of rattler prey this year and since they spend more time digesting in the sun, they're more docile.

Shadows from the desert plants move slowly as we walk and Sun Dream explains the hike to the forest line is over seven miles and there we will take our parts of the sweat lodge. "After a seven mile hike in the desert, the packing of a sweat lodge through two miles of forest, and sitting in a hot hut for an hour or more, all of you will sleep tonight like you haven't since before your children were born." The parents in the group laugh.

After a quarter mile in the desert the other groups break off in different directions from us. They, like us, become single-file processions which set out across the sand leaving any hints of humanity distant and disappearing.

As we walk, Sun Dream answers questions for a time.

"How did you get your name?" someone shouts.

"Mule Deer Fights decided I needed one. I've never had a vision. I'm not supposed to say that, so don't tell them I did, and so he said this would be a good one because I'm beautiful, like a daydream."

"Is he your boyfriend?" I holler.

"Mule Deer? That's ripe. He's Squall Line's boyfriend. Who hollered that?" She looks at me, puts a flattened hand above her dark sunglasses, scrunches up her lip at me.

People ask questions about the actual visions themselves to which Sun Dream repeatedly answers 'I couldn't really say, but I'm told...' or 'what I'm supposed to say is...'

We get to a line in the desert where it changes. The plants become greener, taller, and dunes appear. My ears pop and everyone around me yawns. Up front, Sun Dream rolls her head and cracks her shoulders. My foot lets me know it is there and that the blister still has a few days of pain left in it. But I don't limp: it is no longer enough of a wound to do that to me.

"From here on," Sun Dream says, "we must respect the Indian spirits and proceed without words. Your ears may begin to pop, and if they do it means the Spirits have accepted you. Actually, it means we're going up in elevation. Look, folks, here's the deal. These guys are really hokey with the Indian stuff. I think they make up most of it. And they know nothing about what it really is. Neither do I, but I recognize bullshit pretty easily. So why don't I just not bother with everything they tell me to say and we hike on quietly – trust me on this: it's easier that way – and just do the vision quest as respectfully as possible. Is that okay with you all? You're gonna be tired, hungry, and even thirstier before too long and you need to conserve energy."

The people around me sweat and grit grows on us like mushrooms in a fertilized cave. But Sun Dream seems fine. My own neck and head begin to ache after a few hours. For a while I want water, I crave water, I see water in the desert, water everywhere but here, it surrounds us, encompasses, in every direction it covers the desert. It is like that Coleridge line, 'water, water everywhere, not a drop to drink,' or something. The woman in front of me stops and I run into her. We fall over and I stand, reaching down for her arm. We grab wrists and she stands with a little hop at the end.

"We're going to die of heatstroke," she says to me. "We're all going to die."

"No we aren't, but we'll wish we did."

‹◊›

It is just after two and my heel has started hurting again. Really hurting. But, embracing the pain, I walk at the clip Sun Dream has established. She traverses the trail without problem. I pat my back pocket just to reassure myself that I have some changes of bandages and more topical slime. We walk slowly and my ears pop again. The sand gets steadily thinner and gives way to a long upward slope of gravel and dirt. The path we take is rock surrounded by scree and evergreen bushes. The air is suddenly cooler and the pain in my neck and head fades, returns, then fades.

"Ah, she's the one whose been on your mind off and on today. Well worth it. She's a hottie, she is. And short. I always like the short ones. They have to crouch less, if you know what I mean."

My father doesn't even sweat.

"Don't blame your ill fitness on me," he says. "That's all your mom's side."

"What we're on now is sandstone," says Sun Dream. "I'm actually a geology major at the University of New Mexico, Albuquerque, and am up here doing this for my summer work. This sandstone gives way to shale," she says walking and pointing ahead, "both are sedimentary rocks. Sandstone is sand which was deposited by an ancient ocean millions of years ago, shale was silt from that ocean, smaller particles than sand. Then comes slate,

92

higher up, but it's covered by the forest. This is evidence that the ocean was advancing because the smaller particles are suspended in water for longer and as the water got deeper it moved up the whole plateau area that is the Western U.S. So the rocks you are on now are older than the rocks we'll be on later. This trail goes from shale to forest when we reach five thousand feet. That's where there's enough rain for trees to grow.

"I know I said we'd be quiet, but geology is my thing. Rocks turn me on, what can I say."

The group chuckles. I smile, knowing my in with her. I'll ask about rocks, get her to talk about them. If I can get her to associate me with rocks then every time she thinks of rocks she'll think of me and vice-versa. I stop walking and let my head fall backward, looking through my own dark lenses at cumulus clouds moving in the opposite direction as us. My father says, quietly so no one else can hear, "You're becoming me."

"There are worse people to be like." He scratches his forehead. "Yup, worse people. Take Himmler. He was about as evil as they come. Oh, I know, most people use Hitler as that example but Himmler, he had the choice to follow Hitler or not." He moves his hands in unison, the left following the right. "He chose to follow Hitler. Following, that's always unwise, always puts you a step closer to whatever it is you want to avoid." We continue on, listening to the sounds of the group's feet on the ground. "You're out here trying to find yourself, right? Yeah, I figured so. Ran away from home, right? Yup, good to see you blazing your own trail. Remind me again, whose lead are you following?"

"Yours and grandfather's, alright? Leave me be."

"Looks like someone's vision's begun a little early," says Sun Dream from up front. "Do you need to throw in the towel?"

"No," I say. "I'll be okay. Just let my mind wander too much."

"Is that reason you stopped?" shouts Sun Dream.

"Have a rock in my shoe." I take off the shoe and let dry air touch the blister. I tap the shoe on my other leg. "Got it," I say, hopping to balance while sliding my shoe on.

"Ooh, telling a lie. That's so unlike me," Father's voice, sarcastic, is disembodied.

Sun Dream tells us more about the area's geology, the types of fossils which can be found in the rocks, and that, most importantly, sand is a fallacy and that each grain of sand is really just a small rock. "Geology out here," she says, "is so much different than in Indiana, where I'm from. It's all covered in Indiana and you have to do core samples to find much of the information out. Here you just have to look at the rocks to see what happened." She explains faulting and upheaval to us, how the rocks got like they are and then, without word, we are in the forest's cool humidity. The hike took a lot out of me. It is almost four in the afternoon and I hear my, and other people's, stomachs calling out like a whale, coyote, or other solitary animal trying to end its loneliness.

Inside the forest a few hundred yards are modified backpacks. They hold lengths of plastic tubes or pieces of weathered leather. Large, heavy pieces of leather. Sun Dream stops by the packs and has people pass her. Each person gets one, except me.

"I saw you switch with that other guy. Don't think I haven't seen it before, hot shot. I'm not just some hottie to stare at," she says to me, close, her cheek touching mine, the closeness of her words, the sudden change in the type of sound, makes my ear feel like a cramp.

She stands behind me and says to the group "we must carry the sweat lodge with us. But before we go on we should all take a breather."

"Lunch?" someone asks.

"No food, no water. We're just going to stand for a few minutes and exchange names. You all know mine, so let's go around the group."

"Karl from South Carolina. Construction foreman."

"Joann Roberts, secretary."

"Greg from South Beach, sports agent and antique car collector."

"Barry. I'm blissfully between jobs."

"Marianne. I stay at home with my three lovely children. They're at their grandparents' home this week while my husband Greg," she puts her hand on Greg's shoulder, "and I visit the desert. We've never been here."

"Francine. William's wife." She is the oldest woman in the group. Her hair is gray, face wrinkled, arms floppy.

"William. Retired school teacher. Francine is a retired nurse. We're making the best of our retirement."

"Merak. From Chicago. My family is from out here. I go to college in a few weeks."

"Merak has volunteered, being the youngest here, to carry the two packs with the hut's leather shell."

Sun Dream hands me a backpack and I put it on. It is easily forty pounds of leather inside burlap and nylon. The other one is no lighter and I slide it on to cover my chest. Though the forest is cooler, shadier, and there is a breeze coming down the mountain, my chest and back begin to sweat heavily, my shoulders spasm and after just over an hour I walk hunched like the man evolution missed. Sun Dream is a bitch, one-hundred percent.

‹◊›

"This path is a deer path," says Sun Dream. She looks at me and smiles, happy that I suffer for her. "It is used by a few herd of deer to move about the forest. We will veer off it and to a small lake. There we will find a fire pit where we will construct our sweat lodge. It should only be a half-hour more." She does not have a backpack.

Karl walks next to me.

"Let me take that one off your chest." I stand, groaning, my back cracking and compressing with pain, and he pulls it off, slinging one strap from each bag over each shoulder. "You carried it a lot further than I expected but I don't think you could make it to the site."

"You're right," I manage. The forest air is clean, the sort of clean only found in a pine forest: the smell of the acidic needles and bark pulling foulness from the air. The trees are based by brown circles of needles, no weeds. We go upward slowly but come to a downward slope where the deer trail ends and we have to walk under low branches of pine trees until we reach a lake. It is maybe twenty acres, perhaps slightly more. The water is clear and under the water I can see fish floating, or darting around in formations, a sunken rowboat covered in short coon tail and milfoil.

At the campsite I let the leather slip off my shoulders and fall flat to the ground. Sun Dream comes up to me and kneels. "Don't go out of your way for the scenic view, Merak. You're too transparent for it." Her words are meant only for me and if anyone else heard they do not let on.

Sun Dream shows people how to set up the plastic poles to form the skeleton of the sweat lodge. She takes a round, soot-stained disk with little plastic tubes sticking out of it, a dozen-pointed star, really, and people begin putting lengths of plastic in. As people begin assembling it, their second winds hit and the whole process becomes one of comic mishaps. Soon the star's arms have grown, then again. One arm is too long and a piece is taken off and put on another. The adults talk about adult things, compare where their children were conceived and under what conditions. Sun Dream looks at me as I lie on the ground, my back hurting and shoulders ringed by 550 cords of bruise, something like carpet burns, and pinches which bleed through my shirt. Karl holds his hand down to me. I take it and he pulls me up, holding my back when I get near upright. "Stay tough, brother. She's got a thing for ya or she wouldn't be such a heartless bitch."

"What? That's the most ludicrous thing I've ever heard."

"Some women are like that."

"I traded groups. She thinks I did it just to be in her group, which is true." I lean and pant. "She hates me."

"And you think switching doesn't get her going? No, son, she's into you alright. Chicks dig it when you break the rules for them."

Karl is nuts. Even if he weren't, I haven't put four thousand miles on my car in the last two weeks just for some action. No, I'm here for some major revelation, or whatever, something that makes the eighteen years of my life plus the generations before me make sense. I walk over to the group and help plant the tube ends into plastic holders permanently anchored in the ground. Sun Dream and I unroll a length of leather, which is thin, tough, and a little stiff, and put it on the lodge. It snaps onto one of the frame arms, which is lined by snaps. The next piece of leather snaps onto that one and the process continues. The process ends when the last leather piece snaps to the original one and an eight-foot high dome is built with enough seating for ten people. She sends us out to gather sticks in groups of two. Because there's no one to pair with me, she tells me to stay. Karl winks and gives me an 'okay' sign, just like on my shirt, with his fingers as he and his wife Marianne head into the forest, arms linked.

"I gave you the two bags to see how long you'd hold them. I figured you'd trade one off sooner."

"I didn't know I was allowed. Karl asked to take it because he thought I was going to pass out." For a moment my mind is on a rarified psychic plane and I see exactly how I fit in with the Snyder family: Grandfather stayed for a woman; Father ran and found a woman; I carried two bags of leather for a woman; the realization is like oatmeal in my stomach — Snyder men do what women want, obediently, without questions or independent thoughts. We follow and that is trouble.

"Were you?"

"Probably. Almost passing out seems to be a thing with me."

"I see. I was also punishing you for switching to my group. Not a big deal, I suppose, but still."

"Hot or not, which you are, you're my age and that was why I switched."

My father stands behind her. "Listen to that lie. That's my boy. Ain't no going back now. Welcome to your me-ness."

"And I'm glad you didn't do all the hokey stuff. It's pretty disrespectful to Indian culture for people like Squall Line and Mule Deer to just bastardize it with speeches about spirits and whatever else you're supposed to say."

"You can call them Jeff and Chris around me."

"What's your real name?"

Sun Dream holds out a hand and an index finger and rocks the finger back and forth. "Tsk tsk. I told you my name; it's Sun Dream."

"Your real name."

"What's your real name?" She rolls the sleeves of my shirt up to look at my wounds.

I take out my wallet and show her my driver's license.

"Oh, I see." She smiles at me. "If I'd known those two packs would tear you up so bad I'd have taken one. I'm sorry, Merak."

"It was like forty pounds on each side pulling and turning against each other. It was an industrial-strength Indian burn, is what it was. What the Hell did you think would happen?" I hand her the roll of gauze from my back pocket. She rolls half of it around the wounds on one arm and half around the other, tucking the ends in tightly.

"I just wasn't thinking is all. I'm apologize, Merak, I mean it. That was childish and punitive of me."

"You're forgiven."

People begin walking back in with small pieces of wood. Sun Dream and I go inside the dome and begin setting up the fire. "You know how to set up a fire pretty well."

"I made Life Scout, just a step below Eagle." The fire pit is a cement column with an opening for the wood. On top of it is a metal disk with assorted rocks. I hold one up. "What kind of rock is this?"

"Pumice, lava rock."

"Made of lava?"

"Hence the name. It's molten when shot from volcanoes and lands cooled on the ground. The holes are from escaping gasses. Very light, good heat tolerance, being metamorphic and all."

"Metamorphic?"

"From a volcano."

"Ah, got it."

More people bring in more wood and I set the wood in the firepit, crisscrossing itself.

"I've never known anyone to have a vision on one of these things. Three months I've been here. This is my last week, thank God, but in the whole summer, not one vision."

"It'd be exciting if it happened today."

"If you say so." Evening has set without me knowing it and the smell of the air changes, the feel of it cools. More insects come out and make various noises.

"What kind of rock would you be, if you were one?" I ask.

"That's a standard question; I'd be onyx. Opaque, mysterious, rigid."

"That's how you see yourself? That's not you at all."

"What kind of rock do you think I am, guy who just met me today."

"I don't know a lot of rocks, but I'd say Marble."

"Marble?"

"Yeah. You're pretty, you're reliable and solid, I'm betting," I put my hand on hers "smooth and cool no matter how hot things get."

She looks at my hand on hers. "Well, you wouldn't be marble." She takes it back. "You know a few things about that rock, though."

"My dad's an architect, so I've picked up a lot of stuff on building materials. He knows more about rock facades than anyone at his firm."

"No kidding?"

"No kidding."

"Is he a big architect?"

"Has a bridge he designed in the final three short-list for selection in Kyoto. A major project if it goes. It would be the firm's first major design like that. It's what he wants to do, structural architecture. Mostly they've just done office buildings and expensive homes till now."

"That bridge sounds exciting. What's the firm he works for?"

"Snyder and Cox."

"He owns it?"

I nod.

"Are you an architecture major?"

"I don't know yet. He's gonna let me do whatever I want as long as he sees a use in it"

"That's cool. Geology's actually my second major. I'm mainly an advertising major. My dad is the same way. So I had to take advertising to get him to pay."

A group of people, including Karl, come in with more wood.

"This should be enough," says Sun Dream. She hands Karl a large bucket. "Fill this with water, please."

He takes it, grinning at me as he does, and leaves the lodge. The last of the people wander back in and we sit around the firepit. Sun Dream takes a folded piece of newspaper from her back pocket and hands it to me. I roll it and she lights it with a cigarette lighter. I let it burn a moment then use it to light some kindling and then set it in the wood, which slowly catches fire. I sit next to Sun Dream and we watch the flames age, listen to the wood crackle and tick. Fire spreads from the kindling pieces to the branches in the pit then the logs. Smoke moves in a dark column up through the small opening at the top of the lodge.

When the fire heats enough, Sun Dream closes the flap in the leather and sits back down. She takes the water Karl brought and ladles it onto the rocks, which steam and heat the room. I sit on my section of log, upright, looking at people. Karl takes off his shirt and so do I.

Soon Greg and William have, too. I look at Sun Dream and she smiles at me, winks, takes her sports bra and shirt off, smiles and sets a hand on the log next to me. Karl winks at me then closes his eyes. I put my hand on hers and close my eyes feeling the heat build on me, the steam pulls the last sweat I have from my body. My watch beeps twice and it is seven o'clock. I let myself ease into the darkness of the room, the cracking of the fire, the hiss as Sun Dream adds water to the rocks and the room becomes hotter and wetter.

Then it is cool and there is a breeze. I am naked in a forest of pine trees. The trees are silent except for the sound of the breeze in them. Something calls to me in a language I have heard but do not speak. It asks me to come to it. I do.

The path is lit by an unplaced source. There is no sun, no moon, no stars, just a sky of light, violet dusk. Around, animals watch me. Racoons, hawks, and deer watch me like my childhood babysitter did until her boyfriend would come over and they went up to my parents room to 'talk.' The voice still calls to me, somewhat closer now.

Clouds move through the sky quickly, but the air around me is gentle, pushing and pulling me onward to the voice I recognize but still do not understand.

A river had been calling my name in its language. 'Watch. You have found the answer. You need to find the question.'

The trees continue down a slight incline and up to the wide river. It is shallow, rocky. The rocks are pink and white, beige and black. There is a waterfall, it is small, just four feet high, to my left. I walk into the water, cold, making the skin of my legs tighten. The water breaks on some of the rocks at the base of the waterfall and large salmon jump up it. They ignore me, jump past me, near me, one hits my arm and is pulled back down the waterfall to try the jump again. Across the river a grizzly bear walks out of the forest and looks at me. It looks me up and down. The bear tilts its head askew then, without looking, pulls a salmon out of the air. It tosses the three-foot fish to the ground behind it and grabs another. All still focused on me. It sits on its haunches, takes this second fish in its hands. The salmon fights, squirms, but stops when the bear bites into it, accepting that the bear has changed its path from spawning to being food.

The river tells me the fish feels no pain. It has fulfilled its part of the life cycle. The bear is fulfilling its, too. Animals cannot choose, it says. I feel a hand on my shoulder and it is a woman whose face I cannot discern, but is lovely. She stands behind me, naked, and takes my hand. We stand in the river, holding hands, the small, flat stones of the river under us are smooth and receiving as we watch the salmon and the bear.

The girl pulls on my arm and leads me away from the bear and back to the forest.

<o>

The vision ends when I feel a hand over my mouth and another one shaking me. Sun Dream looks at me and holds a finger over her mouth. The group's eyes are closed. They breathe deeply, in and out at the same time, and no one has a shirt on, not even Marianne or Francine.

Sun Dream and I step quietly outside and we walk down to the lake. She stops at the edge and takes off her shoes. I don't.

"What are you waiting for?"

"We aren't going in there, are we?"

"Yeah. Are you afraid of water?"

"I'm afraid of getting sick. It could be cold. Then there's fish, and algae, too."

"You'll be fine. I do this all the time."

"Sneak out and wade in the water?"

"Something like that."

I take off my shoes, set the gauze from my foot and shoulders on top of a shoe, and walk into the water where she is.

"Weenie," she says, and sticks her tongue out playfully. "My name is Kimberly Lomas. You can call me Kim, but not around them." She thumbs at the leather hut.

"Are humans animals?" I ask her.

"Some of us. Not you."

"You don't know that." I tell her about my vision.

"You're making that up." She splashes me with water. "Oh. No you're not."

"I'm not."

"That's incredible. And some girl was there?"

"I know. That's nuts. Are there supposed to be other people in them?"

"I don't know if there's rules for these things." Kim looks up at me again. "Sit down."

"I'm fine." The water's not too cold, but I don't want to get wet.

Kim reaches up and tugs my shorts and jockeys off, pushing them under water.

"Hey," I say a bit too loudly because Kim shushes me. I turn slightly away from her and pull my soggy clothes back on and sit down a few feet away from her.

"You were just naked in nature, see, and that's part of the vision. What else did you and the girl do?"

"Hold hands."

I reach into the water for her hand. Kimberly watches me as I move and sit next to her.

"Don't be shy. Nothing's going to happen here. It's just nice to sit nearly naked in cool water sometimes. Especially in nature." She leans back so far that her entire body, up to her face, is covered. Her hair floats around her head. Her ears are still above the water, though.

"Okay." I lean backward, too, and rest, ears below water, listening to her steady breaths.

For more than an hour Kimberly and I lie quietly in the chilled air and water, watching the sun go behind the trees and rouge the sky in fanning lines. Occasional deer come to parts of the lake. They look around, some at us, skeptically, and then slowly to the waterfront and drink.

"How are we going to walk back to where we got the hut before ten; it's after nine now."

Kimberly stands. I look up at her and her still toplessness.

Kimberly looks down my body. "You look like you're enjoying this. Don't try to end it."

I blush and look away.

"It's okay, really. If I cared I'd still be clothed in the hut there. But come on. We need to get dressed and back in there before they catch us."

104

We walk to the shore, holding hands for support as much as anything else. Our shirts and socks stick as we put them on, catch on the wetness of our bodies. "How do we get back to the drop spot before ten?" I ask.

"We pack this up and move it to another location. A bus will pick us up and the other groups, too. One of the groups will leave its lodge where we got this one and we'll leave this one where another will get it."

Kimberly and I sneak back into the lodge. She pours a lot of water on the rocks, sending a hot cloud of steam into the enclosure. She leaves some water in the bucket, though. After we sit long enough to build up a solid sweat, she taps people on the knee to bring them out of their meditation, sleep, or whatever else. No one has had a vision, and I say that neither did I.

"You didn't see anything?" Karl asks, winking, looking down at my soaked shorts.

"Nope." And shrug. I pour the remaining water slowly over the last pieces of burning wood. The fire looses steam and an angry cry as I kill it. Water boils on the blackened wood. Kimberly explains to us how to take the lodge apart and pack it up and where it and we will go and that we, thankfully, don't have to walk all the way back to the forest line and only to a dirt road where a bus will pick us up. But we have to do it quickly because we should have begun packing twenty minutes earlier.

Kim and I walk outside of the lodge as the rest of the group stretches and puts their shirts back on. Kimberly leans against a tree and reaches up to my shoulders, touching them gently, running her fingers over the lines of cuts and Indian burn. She pulls my face down and kisses me. Our lips are uncoordinated. Her tongue flicks back and forth across my teeth then between them. The tips of our tongues touch and pull apart.

"You need practice," she says, near my ear. "But you've got some skill. Most good kissers are good lovers," she whispers to me, her face next to mine. "Now go, help take that hut apart."

‹◊›

Karl and I unsnap the leather covering and fold it where it is creased from storage. We pack it into the backpacks it came in, which I carry by choice this time. The skeleton comes apart in seconds and packs just as quickly. The group proceeds out of the fire site, Kimberly and I up front. As night becomes, we reach the edge of the forest. Moonlight drips through the needles of the trees and to the ground. We set the backpacks under a tree ringed with phosphorescent paint and wait a few minutes for a bus to pull up. It is a standard school bus, a too-thin layer of yellow paint covers "District 301" on the side. Kimberly and I take a seat in the middle of the bus. She leans against me. I put my arm around her and lean against the window. Her hands come to rest on my legs. I close my eyes, smile an honest smile, let my breathing slow, and listen to Kimberly sleep and the sound of the bus's tires on the dirt road.

5
Other Sides

The first time I was allowed to drink from actual glass, I dropped it. I stepped on it and a large, incisor-shaped, curve of glass dug into my foot so far the blood came in chunks. Father pulled it out, wrapped my foot in a nearby towel, and drove me for stitches. I remember that pain clearly, the feel of the glass splitting open skin as my weight pressed down without stop, hurting, me tripping and the glass pushing deeper, into one of the abductor muscles. The removal was a relief, an almost pleasurable feel. Years later I stepped on a sliver of glass far smaller than a fingernail clipping and about the width of a thread. It stuck in the ball of my foot. For days it sat there, with every step it pushed in, rammed a hot spot of pain further in to remind me constantly of its thereness. A blister of pus formed over it after a few days and when that popped I soaked my foot in skin-reddeningly hot water until the wound opened far enough for the sliver to sink from it and be gone.

My childhood is like that big piece of glass. It hurts now to think about. And thinking about it is like how I fell on that glass, driving it in further, but there was nothing to stop it – no counter, no wall, no parental arm.

My grandfather's death is more like the sliver, though. Every day I think about it the sadness of missing the funeral tunnels millimeters deeper. That pain twists and changes and where once it was the pain of betrayal – how could my mother say I could not go and how could my father allow that to happen? – it changed to the absence of closure, not being allowed that sense, to its final form: a slow, cooking anger.

High school could have been counted off by the moments of silence led by our principal. Eight, in all. Two in one day, first and eighth hour, for

Mark Grady and Jillian Holiday, the perfect, cute, standard all-American high school sweethearts killed when a car they borrowed hit a horse that had escaped from its stable. They had not been wearing seatbelts, the principal was sure to mention twice. There were two students shot. One plane crash. One football-related burst artery. Two for alcohol poisoning. When my grandfather died, I led my own moment of silence at home, alone in the living room. The clear bowl of fresh potpourri Mother kept on the bar cabinet left the room perpetually smelling lightly of flowers. I sat in the unfamiliar cushions of the living room couch, the couch used only for special guests and holidays, and felt the absolute softness of its deep, like a forbidden jungle deep, cushions. My grandfather's moment of silence could have lasted more than the forty-five seconds the eight students got. I sat and sank, listened to the tick of the clock on the fireplace mantle, heard it chime four times. Outside the bus for the grade school passed, as did a delivery truck. Kids played kickball. But soon the clock disappeared, then the buses, trucks, and kids, too. I sat in a darkness beyond any sense of time and place where my body felt as if supported by something but simultaneously touched nothing.

‹◊›

Kimberly's apartment is sparse. Her clothes are folded neatly into milk crates stacked with the openings forward. In her closet is a single burlap bag, a laundry bag. Her bed is a large air mattress. There is little else, some toiletries in the bathroom, two sets of dishes and silverware, a single pot and a single frying pan. There are no posters nor pictures on the walls, just two postcards, both taped to the wall with a single piece of tape at the top. I flip the cards up and read the backs. They are from a friend of Kimberly's who was in Europe on a study abroad program for eight weeks. The other is from New York and is from the same friend after returning. It says she looks forward to seeing Kim again and claims the side of the dorm nearer the window this year.

Kimberly wakes after me. I had returned to the mattress and laid still, my back to her, looking at the way the morning lightened and blued, feeling supported by nothing as I had when I sat silently for my grandfather. The far side of her apartment is dusty, my feet left tracks in it.

The sun has not yet peeked but the landscape is peaceful, quiet, large birds fly overhead looking for nocturnal rodents late in getting home. Kimberly stirs and I turn to face her. She looks at me for a few seconds, then walks into the bathroom for a shower.

Last night I dreamt of photography. In front of me was a vast landscape of pillars and sand backgrounded by a gold and rose sunset. I raised my camera, focused, unfocused, focused and took the picture. A copy of it appeared in my hand. The picture was clear, an exact replica of the landscape.

The landscape changed to a seascape. Not that I moved, but that after I looked at the picture the lands sank and water rose. The sun moved backward in time to noon and light clouds formed in the sky. The picture of the desert stayed the same. I took a picture of the ocean. I looked at the photo of it and it matched the scene. Ships came in and I took another. The ships turned to skyscrapers, the ocean to streets and people and taxis. Each photo I took remained the same but the landscapes morphed and no matter how many photos I took it was never the same, never even similar, to any which preceded.

Kimberly stands now in the corner of the room by a closet, taking the towel from around her body and wrapping her hair in it, up and into a turban.

"It's your turn," she says, looking into the closet and pulling out a hanging pair of jeans and a white shirt.

When I'm dry and dressed in fresh clothes, I ask her "what gives."

"About?" She sips water from a white cup with faded black lettering.

"Last night."

"What about it?"

"You were all into me out in the woods. Then back here you go absolute zero on me."

"The woods make me horny. Sorry, buck-o, but there's a lot you need to learn."

"So, what, I shoulda made a move there?"

"You didn't, and never can have a chance with me." She pours the last of the glass of water into the drain. "You should really go now."

〈◊〉

It is a long way back to Interstate 70 on the back highways of Utah. I stop at a defunct gold mine for a tour, visit roadside museums and shops which claim to house things like 'the largest prairie dog in the world' or sell 'authentic Indian crafts.' Driving, I make temporary friends. The same couple in the same Chevy station wagon stop at each stop as I. The husband always passes me on the way out. We nod and smile at each other. His name is most likely Abner. He looks like an Abner. His wife looks like an Estelle, or perhaps a Gladys. She has the same hair she has worn since 1954, give or take. She likes dream catchers, wind chimes, and bird feeders. At every stop she buys one of those things. Their house must be curtained by them. Birds of all shapes and species feast there. Hummingbirds to the hummingbird feeders, finches and robins to the smaller feeders, squirrels and pigeons to the larger, and hawks occasionally swoop down and snatch a bird from the air. In the light breeze by their front porch, or perhaps their wrap-around porch, the wind chimes tine, ting, ring and clink as if one hundred and seventy five tiny marimbas are played in unison. The dream catchers must line every wall inside. She is nice, at least, and makes small talk with the clerks, laughs with them and seems to genuinely care about them for the ninety-five seconds they are in her life.

This is why I never talk to her, never make eye contact; each time we stopped she would see me and wave and say "Hi, Merak, how are you at this stop," or "long time no see," and then chuckle as if this were such a clever remark, one unheard by human ears prior to this unveiling. If we passed something like a deer, or a beautiful mountainside, she would comment on it at the following stop, too. Or worse, what if all these curios are gifts and she felt I needed one?

There are also shorter-term friends on the road. Some just pass, quickly, as if they're running from something which threatens to catch them, perhaps does; it may move faster the more they try to run, some predators do that. Some of the cars are in good shape, some pull clouds of blue smoke behind them. One van has no windows, but at least twelve children. They sit and look out the hole where a window once was, fuss with their hair, a sister smacks a brother's head. The man in the passenger's seat sleeps, a line where drool drips and dries from the corner of his mouth and is pulled in a "J" back across his face. The woman driving looks forward, her eyes squinting in the light and dust, and holds the wheel firmly in her hands; she has a single-minded goal: get where she wants to be. No amount of child distractions can stop her. Her journey's intent is antipode that of mine: in the arrival, not the travel.

‹◊›

I arrive late at a motel somewhere in northwest Colorado, some distance off Interstate 70 in a small town called Roan. It is civilization in that there are chain stores and restaurants here, fast food and movies. I have a greasy triple burger, soggy fries and a thirty-two ounce pop in my hands. The burger leaves my fingers, palm to tip, shiny. Two movies are showing, a romantic comedy and an action movie. I opt for the action movie. I sit through it, in the geographic center of the theater, alone for the late show, eating a large, buttered popcorn and drinking semi-flat, too-rich pop from a forty-four ounce cup with extra ice, leaving to deflate my bladder between gun fights. It is almost everything I miss about Chicago and real life – sitting there watching a muscle-bound man jump through windows while shooting down rows of villains lined up because at that confluence of time all of their lives realize their true purpose: good-guy fodder. The shooting ends after one glorious fight where the hero takes bullets in the legs, arms, and chest and keeps climbing and shooting and jumping. He and the villain run out of ammo and, with a final catchy phrase, he pushes the villain into an industrial paper shredder. It is messy. I leave the theater happy, near giddy, throwing out my empty 'Vat O' Popcorn' as if it is a basketball and I a seven-foot center. When it goes in I hold my arms aloft and softly make an "aahhh" sound like a stadium crowd. They are going wild. I spin and there are two movie theater cleaners looking at me. They shake their heads in disapproval. I stop, lower my arms, tug my shirt down twice, and walk past without acknowledging them. They laugh when they think I am out of earshot.

"The crowd goes wild," one says.

I look forward to the comforts of home – friends, television, girls, and a stocked refrigerator. Right now Rick and my other friends are either at the mall or at a park, swinging and talking about girls. They joke about Betty, the mean girl we each had in math class at least once. They lean back, face the sky and hoot at the mention of Rebecca Morgan, one of the junior varsity cheerleaders, who likes being groped, but nothing further. They'd have stopped asking about me days ago, asked my parents where I was and, after seeing or hearing about the note, go about their lives as if I had been planning this trip for months. That is the kind of friends they are: They know when to interfere and when not to.

Or maybe not. I've been gone a long time. I should call Rick, tell him about things, as if he'd understand. He probably wouldn't. He's never questioned much of anything, really, never been forced to. Neither have I, until recently. But there are so many more questions, ones that don't focus on me, ones that focus on others. Like why Anna and Michael have to have such bad lives, why they have to be so poor. They don't deserve it, did nothing wrong. And I did nothing right. But I can afford to go for an impromptu vacation across the country. How is that fair?

But Rick, he's going to a small private college in Massachusetts, one I've never heard of. What they'll teach him that's so much better than a state school, I don't know. Hopefully he won't have to do any deep introspection, ask the questions my father asks my mother all night after a poor kid comes to the door selling magazine subscriptions or generic chocolate.

My mother's answers are always the same. "You worked hard, Richard," they begin. "Because you went to college," "you have a good work ethic," they continue. "I don't know, Richard, I don't know," and, finally, "four a.m. is not the time to talk about the meaning of life, Richard. I'm turning off the light."

Three doors left is a liquor store. I pick up a large, single-can of beer and a fifth of whisky then walk to the register. The clerk looks at me, licks his lips as I walk up to the register and set the alcohol on the counter.

"I.D.," he says, scratching at his thickly-haired ears. A piece of wax dangles from his long, tan fingernail and he wipes it on his pants.

When I was young my father worked at a firm he did not own and had his boss over for dinner. A project was coming up that my father wanted. He introduced me and we, the boss, my father, mother and I, sat down at the dining room table. The adults talked about different things, one of which was the boss's beard.

'I've thought of growing a beard,' my father said. 'How do you clean them?'

'Shampoo. It's hair, is all, shampoo keeps the beard soft.'

'Do you shampoo your ears, too?' I asked. My father did not get the assignment.

I pull out my wallet and hand him a driver's license. He looks at me, and it, rubs at the birthday with his thumbnail and says "I'm sorry, Mr. McGee, you look young for twenty-three."

"Shampoo." I shake my head. "Sorry, what I meant to say was, I get that a lot. My frat brothers," I go out on a limb, "make me do beer runs every Friday because they think it's funny that I get carded every time, even by clerks who know me."

His looks asks what 'shampoo' means, but he says, "Frat boys, gotta love it. Enjoy college, Brian, life goes downhill afterward."

I take my alcohol back to the Roan Motel and proceed to drink the beer. I only rarely drink. Usually, I buy for friends, like Amy, who has a keen love of fruit wines. The can is cold, heavy, and I hold it letting the cold filter into my palm and when my fingers numb, I take the tab under my nail and let the 'sshh' from the can. I sip it till it warms, then finish it, and as I do I write about Abner and Gladys (I decided) and the rest of my temporary friends and draw maps approximating where I am and how I drove here.

〈◇〉

This morning, now, the Roan Motel room is cool, nearly cold. The air conditioner is on high and in the windows of my room float continents of condensation. My head is a little sore from the weak hangovers I get on the occasions when I drink. I take two Aspirin and drink a lot of water, knowing I'll be drinking later as the whisky is not yet open.

The sink and mirror are in the bathroom of this room, a pleasant change from the Motel in Page, and I stand in front of them pulling my shirt collar up with my tie draped around my neck.

"No, son, the thin end on your left, broad on the right." Father is in the doorway, paging through the hotel television station list. "There's only one adult movie station here, and only two movie channels. Did you notice that? I'd expect more from satellite."

"Thin end left?"

He walks up behind me and takes my hands in his. "Pinch the tie here and here. The broad end wraps around the thin twice, but don't let it fold any. Then the broad part comes up behind, yes like that, through the hole between your neck and the tie, and then down through the wrapped

114

part. There. Pull it tight." He pulls it then adjusts the back of the tie so it's fully behind the front. "Not a Windsor knot, but it works."

"Good enough for church, you used to say."

"Yup. Should be good enough for my dad, too."

I look at his reflection, our eyes meet for the first time in months. "How did you know?"

"Why else would you be here?" He steps back to the doorway. "Got your tie clip?"

"I forgot it."

"Well," he says turning and heading into the room, "you'll have to do without. There may be a safety pin around, need be." He takes a last look at the suit, up, down, pausing at the ankles and wrists. "You need a new one."

My only suit, at three years old, is too short at the wrists and ankles, and hugs my crotch in a way which borders between cozy and angry. It and the shirt come up my arm about four inches and up my legs more than a half-a-foot. It was bought for me to wear to my grandfather's funeral. My mother, however, would not let me go because the funeral was during finals week. My father went alone. This suit should have also been for church, but I haven't gone since my grandfather died. Not because my grandfather died, but in protest that it couldn't wait a week. In the suitcase that held my suit is the folded letter grandfather sent me before he died. It is in its original envelope addressed in his alternately thick and thin jagged lettering. The return address is the address and plot number of his graveyard. I set the letter in my spiral notebook, replacing the pencil place marker, and walk out to the main office. The grave is in a little town called Piceance, so small no map has it, but it is less than twenty miles from Roan.

At the front desk, two women sit, talking while doing paperwork. One sits on the yellowish granite counter, popping gum, tapping the heel of her flat against the front of the counter while talking about other employees; her voice comes from deep inside; though nasally, it carries out of the office and down the corridor where I walk. The other is behind the counter, nodding, laughing, and entering data into a computer. When I walk in to the lobby the woman on the counter hops off and greets me. I walk to her and the other and set the envelope down.

"Do you ladies know where Piceance is?"

The one who had been talking looks at my suit, at the sleeves and cuffs, the legs and how my socks cover the gap between my ankles and the hems. Her lips contort in a frown as she tries not to laugh. The other woman takes the envelope and looks at the address.

"Piceance, yeah, about twenty miles north. You're looking for Saint Atheneum's, the church." She points to the road the hotel is on and says to follow it to Piceance and go right before the stoplight. "Saint Atheneum's is on the left, it kind of stands out."

"You know the area well," I say.

She brings her hand to the counter and taps her ring finger on the surface, there is a silver engagement ring. "I'm a congregant."

"Well, fantastic," I say. "Is there a place in town I can buy some flowers?"

She points to a gift shop across the street.

"Thank you for your help."

Back at my room I get a clean shirt and khakis as well as a bucket of ice, one of the bathroom's glass (glass!) tumblers, and the whisky. I put them on the passenger's floor and drive north across a plateau of scrub and sage punctuated by occasional small mountains and stands of haggard trees.

'I grew up in the desert, son.'

My father sits in the passenger's seat. He wears a suit, too, and looks out at the scenery. Where my suit is a tailored off-the-rack, his is custom-tailored, as they all are. It is black with medium gray pinstripes. The shade of gray is eighteen percent gray, the exact middle tone of gray. It's the approximate shade of gray that both red and green take in monochrome photographs. His tie is solid black and his shirt white. He wears the tie clip mother gave him for their tenth anniversary; he wears it every day. It is silver with a single dark sapphire on the end.

'You'd think I'd like it out here, that seeing these hearty plants would warm the bottom of my heart and remind me of my childhood. They do, and I hate them for it. Fucking Yucca. God's ugliest damned shrub, if you ask me. Even uglier than Aloe or that shelf-like fungus that grows on dead trees.'

"It's not so bad here. A sort of, of, what's the word?"

'Austere.'

"Yes. Austere. It has that kind of beauty to it."

'If I push you away like my dad did me, you have to keep after me, don't accept it like I did.'

I turn to look at him, to promise I will do things differently, but father is gone.

‹◊›

Piceance is a town without a population, just an elevation, according to the sign, of 9,752 feet. It begins without looking like a town and is just some older buildings with the names of local companies. There's a contractor and quarry, two ranch entrances, and a nice cedar-sided home directly opposite a cement-walled, metal-roofed building with a car port.

The town itself is a one-light, one-intersection town where two state highways meet, the unmarked north-south one I am on and the east-west highway fourteen. There is a Sinclair gas station. The fiberglass dinosaur out front is adorned with tack and bridle. The saddle is worn, and perhaps many people stopping here for gas have had their picture taken riding the dino. Across from the gas station is a restaurant, diagonal a curio shop, and opposite a video rental store which is not a chain. The town has a dentist's office and a doctor's. They share a building and a banner which says "Ranch Calls on Tuesdays and for Emergencies."

Saint Atheneum's is a large, white building with dark timbers trisecting the outside. It looks out of place for the town but fits the dense pines and mountainsides around it. The cemetery is behind a tall, wrought fence with brick posts every twenty yards. The size is vastly disproportionate to the population of any one-light town. Inside is a parking lot for up to twenty cars and a small octagonal gatehouse. The outside is sided in cedar planks, the roof thatched with slate shingles. I park next to it along with three other cars. Inside it are seven pink granite walls. Brass tags are fixed to the rock. They are in chronological order of arrival, back as far as 1806, and list grid numbers. On the wall just right of the entrance is a four-foot by four-foot map of the cemetery, with a grid. I find my grandfather's name. He is buried in G8 B6. There is a red dot on the map for the gatehouse and entry lot. I trace the road up to his plot, it is halfway up a tendonous cul-de-sac branching off the main road. I drive from the small parking lot and follow the road and occasional signs (G4-G10, Go Right; later: B1-B6, Go Left) to G8 B6.

What my grandfather's connection to this church is I'll never know. The site is on the side of a hill. It overlooks the church's stained glass Christ, Dove, and Light and has a small view of the town of Piceance and the traffic light. It is too far to see anything but occasional cars pass through the intersection or stop and wait for the light to change. They pull into the gas station, park for a while, then pull out. Some parallel park along the street and stay there. On two far slopes are small white squares; homes, quiet, I imagine, family-like, peaceful. Dogs play in the backyards, fathers and sons toss frisbee; mothers have tea with the neighbor women and talk about whatever it is they have to share. Or at least that's how it should be. In reality it must not be much different from my own life where fathers and sons work on the father's hopeless, swaybacked, inresusciteable sports car bought for under ten grand from someone who had spent fifteen years trying to make the engine do something; the father, angry that the new header doesn't fit correctly, throws it into the wall leaving a hole in the Sheetrock and an outward bulge in the aluminum siding. The mothers work on the landscaping, weeding the vines that grow under the siding and planting new annuals. A service comes in and sprays chemicals on the grass after mowing it and the pets are kept indoors, coddled, groomed for presentation at the nightly walk when all the neighbors 'coincidentally' walk their dogs at the same time. The prize dog would be a German Shepherd with a rare tint and a picture-perfect physique from three doors down. Or perhaps the blue French Poodle from Pine Circle or the Labrador with the personality bred out of her. Then these peoples' lives would be recognizable.

I step from my car, roll the window down and lean against the roof. The hill is gentle, well-tended with rows of hedges and flagstone steps and paths. To my grandfather's right is my grandmother, Lily Hillary Snyder, 6/3/1926-1/3/1979. Beloved mother, teacher, and ecologist. Killed early by a drunk driver. Her stone is black, the grooves of the letters slightly rounded, the stone's surface smooth but not like grandfather's. Quentin Dudley Snyder, 2/2/1907-6/7/1994. Loving husband and carpenter. Lost to cancer. His stone shines, is smooth like a mirror. The letters are squared, the edges straight and severe. Outside their stones are columbine groupings; between them is a thin band of grass and on it I set the flowers. I sit behind them and look at the church, feel the grass on my legs and butt, the chill breeze move around me and in occasional, stronger moments move the tops of the forest around the cemetery.

The grass is cool – the plots are in the shade of tall, venerable trees. I set the bottle of Jack down next to grandfather's gravestone and put some ice cubes in the tumbler. The seal of the plastic around the bottle cracks at the serrations as I twist the cap off. The light brown stuff, strong, not something I enjoy, rides the cemetery breeze to my nose as I pour a few ounces over the cubes. Foggy lines crack into the clear blocks.

The suit legs ride past my socks, arms near my elbows. The breeze comes up the legs and across my forearms. It is not an unwelcoming thing, but would also not allow people where they don't belong. I take the letter out of the envelope.

"I got your letter, Grandpa. I didn't really understand it before. Or maybe I did but didn't want to, or some such thing. I do now, though. Everything was laid out here. I'm gonna read it, so you can remember what you wrote." The small stationary sheets he always used are off-white with tan fibers. The edges are brown from handling, dark from readings and re-readings, most spent trying to discern what was written under the heavily crossed out lines he must have felt me unready to know.

March 17th, 1994

Dear Merak,

One of the many aspects of childhood is that of questioning. Only when the questioning stops do you truly become an adult – a state of affairs no one should ever have to suffer through. I know you have a lot of questions you are unaware of, some of which I am willing to answer.

I wish you could have known your grandmother, such a lovely person. She was very much like you, Merak. She never stopped questioning things, though, and in that regard was never fully burdened by adulthood. Let me tell you about how it is I came to know Lily.

I was almost fifty-seven and had decided on a life of permanent bachelorhood when I met your grandmother. When I was fourteen my parents decided to move to Los Angeles. My brothers Isaac and Jacob decided to go with them, I had my heart set on staying because I was in love with a girl named Carol, she was an Indian, I forget the tribe name, and lived inside the Grand Canyon.

She was willing to marry me, leave everything, but I had to be willing to adapt to her ways of life, too, and I was too immature to do that. I don't know what I thought she meant by 'adapt,' but I wanted her to live the sort of life I recognized, one I could show to my family as just like ours so they'd accept her. Or I thought that would be what they'd accept. They would have taken her as she was, Snyder's do that, but I didn't have much faith in my parents and brothers.

After she left my life I took frequent hikes into the Grand Canyon, usually hidden or non-existent trails. Perhaps I wanted the chasm to kill me so I wouldn't have to do it myself, I don't know. On a hike down a new, tourist-friendly path I met a woman at the mid-point. She was sitting on a wood bench resting against a dynamited-out section of canyon wall, dripping water on her head. She was dressed very unladylike in jeans – of all things! – and boots. Not so uncommon a site for you, I presume, but back then, where I lived, in the brief time between Korea and Vietnam, it was quite a shock. I, of course, was curious and sat next to her without asking. Her name was Lily, she said. She was new to the area and an avid hiker. I immediately assumed her to be a lesbian, though we didn't call them such things back then, until she said she was glad to have dumped her last boyfriend who was not a hiker at all.

We hiked back up and I'll tell ya, boy, I was fit but she was walking circles around me. She had a college education from out east and taught algebra and geometry at a nearby school for Indians. So happens Carol's young children would go there just a couple years later. But I never saw Carol again, myself.

Well, anyway, Lily was no stranger to a man's touch, which shocked my conservative Lutheran beliefs (ones which only applied to women, anyway,) but I got over it pretty fast. And soon she was pregnant with your father. We got married a few months later. For our honeymoon we went on a camping trip to a slot canyon called Antelope Canyon; should your mother ever let you come visit me, I'll take you there. We also went to Monument Valley, Zion National Park and Bryce Canyon. Spent two or three days in each. We had gotten a car, a semi-used Chevy, from her side of the family as a wedding gift. It was driven down to us by her father, a lawyer from Boston, and mother. At the reception my father got drunk – shocking to me being that he never allowed alcohol, or anything with alcohol, in the house when I grew up. He stood up and said 'Quentin, good work on keeping the Snyder family tradition alive' then fell over.

Confused by this, I asked my mother after the wedding what it meant. My whole life my parents had lied to me about the year they married, you see. She explained that I was an accident. That when she found out she was pregnant she and my father went to the city hall and got married so I'd never have to know that I was an accident, too. Perhaps then the Snyder tradition would end. My father had been an accident, as had his father, grandfather, and who knows how many others. Your father was born about five months after Lily and I married.

He realized this when he was about your age. He'd never known how long Lily and I had been married but asked one day, and I told him, foolishly, the correct year instead of adding one as I should have done. He looked at me and asked if I got married because of him. I didn't know what to say. I'd somehow talked myself into believing he'd never ask. So I said yes, but that it would have happened anyway, just not as quickly. He took it badly, very badly, and left the house. He didn't come back for five days. When he did, and he will never tell you this story so forget you hear it now, I told him he was no longer welcome in the house and that was the last we talked for six years. He went to college, got married, and you were an infant before we spoke again. It was Lily's death that got us speaking again. She had never shut him out and for six years had tried to get me to let him back in my life, that your father needed it, but I wouldn't speak of it. I was so, so ignorant.

I don't know why your mother hates me so much, but she does. She was against me ever coming back into your father's life. Sometimes I think she doesn't really care for any Snyder except you. You could probably tell this yourself from family reunions. I don't know why this is so, but I stopped questioning it years ago.

Looking for answers to these types of questions is like hunting jackalope: you'll never bag one because they don't exist; you may find them, however, when they're ready to present themselves to you.

Your thousand questions, the ones in your mind now, will answer themselves in their own time and bring with them questions you had not thought of before. Such is the way of things, Merak. The question behind all of this is too big to ask, let alone answer. You know the question, we all know our question, but in God's sense of irony there is no way to voice it sufficient to answer.

There is just one last thing I have to say, Merak. You must keep this letter in confidence insolong as I live. This won't be long. My lifelong fear of the doctor has caused me to realize my lifelong fear of death. I've got cancer and it's spread to about every organ and system in me. I've only got a month, maybe two. I will hold out as long as I can, perhaps when I tell your parents they will let you visit me. Maybe I won't be able to take you to Antelope Canyon after all. Such wishes are those of a man who has not accepted his imminent mortality.

Love always,

Grandpa

I fold the letter and slide it back into the envelope. "I'm sorry I've been so long in coming." The cemetery is quiet. There are other people at graves. They kneel at tombstones, somehow supplicant. They visit, place their flowers, look around uncomfortably and leave. They are thieves, invaders, robbers of the solitude of the dead. Perhaps they realize this: the dead do not wish living companionship and visiting graves is a violation of that wish, a selfish act of self-solace. Some stay as long as fifteen minutes, others as little as five. Some act afraid, afraid of the fact that we all spend the majority of our existences interred.

A car passes, leaving the cemetery. It is going faster than the posted fifteen mile-per-hour speed limit. "I worked on a letter of my own. I understand now what the family tradition is, and that I'm as much part of it as my father. I'm just an idiot not to have seen it sooner. No, that's not right; I just didn't want to see it sooner – and still wish I didn't. I suppose one of these scratched out lines says it's up to me to break the tradition. It's always up to us, then to our children, to change things, isn't it? Every generation drops the ball, doesn't it?" I open the notebook to the first page. "I've been keeping track of my trip and I want to tell you about it. I was just going to sum it up, but I know you always liked a good story. Maybe this one's good enough, I don't know."

I read starting with day 1, July 31st, 1997, "I left the house today. Leaving wasn't easy like I planned. I stopped outside and looked back at it; the brick facade, at the Chemo-Green lawn, the perfectly trimmed hedges, the way the sidewalk sections all line up; and was torn by two strong feelings. On one hand I found that the picture-perfect suburban life suited me and I didn't want to leave it. I wanted to run inside and be seven and ride my bike and play with my action men and ask my parents every night when I could have a baby brother. Then I felt ill. Ill because the outside of the house, of every house lining the development's streets, it seemed, held flaws behind the double doors. The Mitchells, their father paying for the abortion for their sixteen-year-old babysitter who was pregnant with her wards' half-sibling. Six doors the other way the Ferguson wife and children had been seen a number of times with bruises above their hem lines. And each year everyone came out to the retention basin in the center of the development for a picnic and informal competition on how much more perfect their lives were than anyone else's. And I wanted it to be over and every lie I knew of to be open, public knowledge, and the buildings to crumble, weeds to grow, and the sidewalks to upheave until the neighborhood reflected the 'families' there. But they aren't all bad. Some of the people there are honestly caring, loving people who put time into the PTA for reasons other than to show off the new sweater they bought that month.

"As I stood there, though, memories came back like movies and I saw all the moments in my life that influenced who I am. There was me with my bike – without training wheels, driving the Volare for the first time, trying to get the Ferrari to turn over while father held some pieces together, then others. They layered like stacked slides." I tell him about the weeks after seeing mom at the mall and the car ride home and how father is fine with the affair and how I've wondered if he has a girlfriend, too. I tell him about St. Louis and the bad drivers there, about Oklahoma and Texas and two jackhammer thunderstorms I had to drive in, about outrunning a tornado that was in a field to my right. About Arizona and the Grand Canyon. About Anna. "You'd have liked Anna. Been drawn to her as I was. We're more alike than I'll ever know, I figure." I show him the diagram of the blister. I continue through the forty-or-so pages I have written so far. As I do I sip the glass of whisky empty, refill it, sip it empty again, put more ice in and repeat. I read out loud past the point where my voice tires and fails.

When I finish I close the notebook, the envelope inside of it. "I've seen why you loved it out here so much." The bottle of Jack is a third empty. My voice is quiet, quieter than the cicadas, birds, and air; I listen to the breeze on the leaves, the way I inhale it, and the buzz of my nervous system. Laying back into the grass and tree shade, the bottle of Jack falls when my leg hits it, but the world spins pleasantly and I don't want to change that. I close my eyes, pass through twilit visions of the Ferrari's lights turning on and my father taking us all out for pizza to celebrate, my parents finally deciding, after years of work, on a church they could both agree upon that at once catered to the conservative upbringing my father had and my mother's Unitarian upbringing. There was Rick standing over his car's bifurcated remains, asking who was driving it and why the person he leant it to was giving the keys to someone else at the party. Two days later, Rick standing next to me for Mark Grady's and Jillian Holiday's moments of silence. Rick and I at Denny's starting a food fight and running up the parking lot embankment and across Interstate 94 when the police arrived. My parents pulling the popcorn popper from the cupboard below the silverware drawer and emptying quarter-cup after quarter-cup into it until the five gallon bowl had filled, then topping the exploded kernels with the fluid yellow of two-thirds of a stick of melted butter and salt. Amy and I on our first date, a short relationship, too young to drive, my father and mother going dutch with us. That was back when Colander was still the spare car. Father plans to make it his next project car. When I wake, the sun is in mid-set and the moon is a red hemisphere on the horizon.

The gravestone is warm, having taken in the sun all day. "Dad, he's such a dick, Grandpa. And mom's no better. I mean, they could have done a better job breaking this news to me. They could have avoided hiding it from me when I was a kid." I tap the gravestone. "That's the way to do it, Gramps, and if this happens to me, if I become dad like you and all the other Snyder men, I'm gonna do it different. I'm gonna be open with the boy and he's gonna know what happened and that way he can cope before some big thing happens like this. Yup, that's the way to do it."

The wind is my grandfather, a soft background stirring, never absent. "I wish I could talk to you right now, to find out what it's like up there." I start to say 'in Heaven', but stop, as if it would be bad luck to presume. "Reverend Beckett used to say confusing things about what happens when we die: people who don't go to church go to Hell; people who don't believe go to Hell; people who aren't Christian go to Hell. He didn't seem like a Methodist. I hear he's toned down, now. He would say there's all these rules and stuff to meet to get into Heaven and only those who follow them get in, but then next week would say how anyone who believes gets in. I guess he was really just telling us no one really believes. Anyway, I hope that when you got there you learned some of the answers to those big questions and such not, the ones dad stopped asking years ago.

"You two must have loved each other a lot. It's easy, in this family, to go from love to hate, it seems." When I was seven, the church brought in Reverend Beckett. His first sermon spoke of how Satan was part of God's plan and while we may not understand it all, God needed Satan's evil to show how good God is. Father explained it in the car ride, because I was confused and scared by the idea that the Spirit of Love described in Luke needed to cause hatred and pain.

"Love and hate, Merak, they're like heads and tails on a coin."

"Love and hate are the same?"

"Are the heads and tails on a coin the same?"

"Richard, you're confusing him."

"Margaret, he needs to figure this out. I'm helping. Are the heads and tails the same?"

"No"

"What are they?"

I shrugged.

"Are they on the same side?"

"No. Opposite sides."

"So they're opposites, right?"

"Yeah."

"But part of the same coin, right?"

"Yeah."

"And when a coin is on the table, how many sides are visible?"

"Richard, where is this going?"

"Margaret, Good Lord, shut up. Merak, the coin?"

"Only one side shows. Except on our table, because it's glass."

"Right, but if the table's not glass, how many sides?"

"Just the one."

"Think of that coin as the world, or people, Merak. The world has a lot of good, and people have a lot of good, but the world and people have a lot of evil in them, too. There are both sides and what people need to do is keep the good side up, the evil side to the table, just like only one side of the coin can face out, so, too, can only one side of a person. Which side is your mother showing right now?"

These two sides, they flip so haphazardly. "I don't know which side my father's going to put forward when I see him next, Grandpa. But people don't just put one side forward, it's so much more complex than that. Especially with this family where love and hate become one so readily.

"I need to go home now." The bottle has spilled and I pour the rest of it out, dump the bug-islanded water the ice bucket has become, too. "I imagine dad and mom are worried, or mad, or both, and I hope that dad doesn't cut me out. You warned me about doing just this. You knew I wouldn't listen. I guess some warnings aren't about deterrence – they just let you know the consequences."

I touch each gravestone again, "I'm sorry I never got to know you, Grandma," then leave.

‹◊›

The restaurant by the traffic light is "Buffalo Gil's." It looks like an old-style saloon with a seating area in the front lined by hitching posts, bench swings by the front door, wind chimes every fifteen feet along the roof. I park in front of a souvenir store next to it and stop there before getting food. Inside are the clocks made of petrified wood, wall hangings of fossils, the most expensive of which looks to be forged because the animal, clearly a lizard, has no pelvic structure. Display cases of locally-quarried crystal, jewelry, and loose 'gems' line a far wall. A cart of tumbled rocks is near a life-sized wood Indian and a glass display tower with spires and shapes of polished desert rocks, small pewter miniatures, and smaller miniatures hand glued onto common rocks. Some are horses, others ducks, dragons, wizards, or buffalo. All have small gem chips for eyes. A pewter cow on a white quartz crystal with red eyes makes me laugh.

"Can I help you?" says a man's voice from behind a bead curtain.

"How much for the devil cow?"

The man walks into the front room. He has a wood cane, the grip is a carved face with a beard that goes a third of the way down the shaft. "All the miniatures are seven dollars."

I take a ten from my wallet. "Do you ship?"

"Three fifty, anywhere in the country."

I add a single and write my address on a mailing label. "Thank you much," I say as I leave. The man waves goodbye. I walk across the street to the restaurant, my stomach has finally let me know it wants to eat. Though the edges of the world are still bleary and tomorrow I will be hungover, food sounds like a survivable necessity. Every meat on the menu is buffalo, ostrich, or alligator. I order a pop and a buffalo burger – rare, on a hard-top roll, lettuce, and fried shoestring onions. I open my notebook to a new page and ask the waitress for a pencil. She gives me one from her apron.

Today, no. Every one of my entries begins with 'today.' I cross it out and try On this day, but that's the same. I cross it out and begin again.

I visited my grandparents. I was there for hours telling them about my trip and how I ran away just like my father did. I got fairly drunk and fell asleep through most of the afternoon and evening. I needed it.

Their headstones were cut from the same rock, I imagine. Their graves were the kind of place I want to be buried when I die. The cemetery was huge, the church small. Their plots overlooked this small town called Piceance and the intersection with the restaurant I'm sitting at right now. Before I sat down I bought a pewter cow, about an inch tall, on a piece of quartz. It's possessed and funny.

The waitress sets my burger, onions, and pop down. When I lift the burger from the plate three drops of juice fall onto the notebook. It tastes like a regular burger, only gamier.

I don't know what this running away says for my future, though. Like father said, my reaction would speak volumes on the type of man I will become.

I circle drops of juice which hit the paper and write "Please forgive the buffalo juice."

6
The Great Divide

Lightning flashes and fifteen seconds later there is a rumbling thunder which begins like a hungry stomach and ends shaking the ground. It is just before three a.m. and I lie in my sleeping bag at a rest stop near a small creek. Sitting on me are one hundred and seven frogs. Some doze, some watch me. They seem content to be there and I'm fine with them. There are all kinds of frogs. Some are smaller and some are spade-shaped or shaded with variant green hues, others are wide and bull-eyed. One is pale, near white, with large hips which poke his skin outward like posts do a circus tent.

Soon the lightning flashes more frequently and a close strike sets to honking the alarms of two cars. Frogs begin hopping off, hopping into nearby trees or just away to darkness. The rain starts as a simple, random, intoxicating drop on my lips. It's cold, and for a while I listen to the soft lullaby of gentle rain hitting the leaves of the trees overhead. When the lightning gets closer, thunder sharper, and rain harder, I shoo the last half-dozen frogs away, grab my notebook and pencil from the ground, and stand quickly. Rain approaches like a cymbal on the road.

I set the sleeping bag on my trunk and roll it. Rain hits the notebook; circles appear and shine on its cover. I work with the trunk, turn the key, grip the spoiler, hit the top and back of it, but when it doesn't open and I feel the cold air of the harder rain sweep the ground, I give up and toss my notebook and sleeping bag in the back seat. Colander is testy from age and recent use, not malice. My father has owned malevolent cars, the Ferrari for one, the Saab for another, cars that would simply not work because they felt like it. Colander is a loyal car and loyal cars do not cause problems without reason.

I turn on the radio and there is a state-of-emergency for areas east of me and Interstate 70 is closed at around exit 173 due to a massive landslide. Further, a dam in the north of the state has broken and the announcer lists off towns in the path of the coming flood. I decide to leave anyway. There will be detours.

There is a niceness in driving in pre-dawn rain. The sound of the water hitting Colander, cleansing it of the last three weeks' dust, erasing Anna's hands from the roof. For a split second, after each wiper pass, the occasional oncoming car is clear, but then again two white dots surrounded by large, diffuse circles of light. The wipers, on high, click twice for every word the radio announcer says about the road closures. Occasionally, police or ambulances speed past me with their lights on, pulling a tail of water. At the next exit I pull off and stop for directions.

My homecoming, when I get past this rain and the other states, will be like any day, I imagine. I'll walk in sometime around lunch, or the early-afternoon at worst, unpack Colander and take my film to be developed. I'll pick it up an hour later and have it ready to show my parents. Father will come home first, which he does if my mother has spent the day out of the house, and he'll say hi, as if I hadn't been gone for three weeks, because he may not notice the absence, ask where my car has been all this time and go out to the garage to work on the Ferrari. In the family room I'll power on the video games and for an hour or so be a privateer, or commando, or mushroom-munching plumber. Then mother will come home and give the customary hug and take three green boxes of dinner from the freezer. She'll have to read the directions, she always has to read the directions, and set them in the microwave one at a time to cook. As we eat, blowing on the crisped edges of the broccoli or green beans before biting them, they'll ask how my trip was and I'll say 'just fine.' I'll take out the pictures and we'll go through the rolls, which in time will become boring because there are only so many different pictures of the desert someone can look at before getting bored.

They'll ask about the people, like Anna and Michael. And I'll say they were friends I met along the way. Travel-friends. Father will announce that his bridge either won, or has been accepted to the top two designs, and that he knows how to make the Ferrari live. We'll clap and Mother will stay oddly silent about what she has done for the last three weeks.

Near the highway is a small beacon of light. Next to a closed gas station is an open convenience store. Clerks at these places always know the area and the directions for hidden passages. I park in a spot near the door and run in, my hands over my head as if that would keep off any of this rain. When the door clacks shut, ending the percussion of rain and thunder, the shoulders and back of my shirt are wet, as are my pants legs and shoes, which squish like mud.

Inside is a plump, gray-haired man reading a magazine front-covered by a bikini-clad girl holding cigars and back-covered with a man on a horse, smoking a cigarette, roping a calf. The clerk shoves it under the counter and straightens his uniform shirt.

"I'm sorry. Didn't see you coming."

"No prob. I used to work at a place like this. In Chicago," I add to assure him I'm not with his company, if this is a chain.

"You know the game, man, you know it."

"Ah, yes, I know 'the game', as it is." I walk to the coffee counter. "Can you brew a pot of your strongest stuff?"

"Not allowed to until five a.m." He points at a wall clock with a sign under it. 'No fresh coffee until 5:00 a.m. NO EXCEPTIONS.' Under that is a handwritten note reading 'exsept for cops and pairametics.'

"But, I know 'the game.'"

"So you know why I can't do it."

"That's only twenty minutes off, man. Come on."

"The game has rules, man; the game gots rules."

"Come on, buddy, you can bend 'em."

He shakes his head and looks around the store.

"I'll buy two large coffees. Most of the pot. You can pour what's left into one of these older pots." He looks at me; he's thinking about it. I pull two large coffee cups from the dispenser and put cream and sugar into one. "Should I cream and sugar this second one?"

"Aw, heck, go ahead."

I know the game, the rules, the strategies, the ways to win. After prepping the other cup I grab a newspaper from a rack by the door.

"This week's may be late, what with the road closed up and all."

I look at the front page and there is a picture of Antelope Canyon and a bunch of Ambulances around it. Paramedics pull someone on a backboard out of an unassuming slit in the ground. There is a helicopter behind them. The caption says "Antelope Slot Canyon tragedy, page 4." Page four is headed with a second picture, that of three bodies on the ground, each covered with a sheet. A mongrel dog's nose is under one of the sheets.

The tragedy at Antelope Canyon a week-and-a-half ago is still being investigated. Already families of the drowned have begun filing law suits. At 12:07 p.m. on Thursday, August 12th, a flash flood from mountain rains earlier in the day washed into the Antelope Canyon outwash. There was no warning, said the survivor, a local boy. "There was just this loud noise, and I did what I always heard to do – pressed against the wall and prayed."

According to the survivor, the other hikers panicked when they heard water. "I kept shouting for them to press against the walls. They panicked and thought they could climb out. I begged them to listen but they kept climbing," he told police when he was rescued later that day. He was found naked, buried in mud to his shoulders in a section of canyon off-limits to most tourists. Bodies of the twenty-three missing hikers are still being recovered from an underground lake.

The entrance to the lake, a downward hole in the cave, is hampering efforts because no search equipment can be brought in to search the water. Additionally, the cave presents no easy means to anchor lifts to retrieve victims.

"Floods aren't uncommon this time of year," said geologist Hillary Roberts, an expert on the canyon. "Usually, they can be predicted, however. This was a fluke because the rain causing it occurred so far away."

Though investigations are ongoing, it is believed the operators of the canyon will bear no ultimate blame and in fact told the tourists about bad weather in the mountains and their warnings went unheeded.

I read the article over and over again. Watersharer said The Universe would look out for me; because of Anna I left the Grand Canyon a day early and visited Antelope canyon a day earlier than I may have, exactly twenty-four hours before this flood. And I would have panicked, climbed for the top. The top only fifty feet up, the colliding and collapsing sound of fast water, having a tenth of a second or less to see the brown-red wall before it hit, pulling people off the canyon and making them pieces of debris. The Universe, it seems, is watching out for me.

Shivers run from my feet up and forehead down, meeting and passing in my gut. I touch the dog on page four; it could have been sniffing me. But it was not. And not for a long time will I be the body under the sheet. I know it like I know two-plus-two is four or that an apple is red and an orange is orange. It is common sense.

"That news is all old," says the clerk.

"I was at this canyon once."

"No shit?"

"No shit."

"Coffee's up."

I set the paper on the counter. "I'd like to buy this, too."

"K."

I buy my coffees and the paper, three dollars even.

"You know any way around that road closure–" I look at his scratched name tag "Randy?"

"Ron D. And yes, the road this here store's on, just follow it that way," he points, "and in about fifteen miles ya come to a bridge. Go over it and you'll see some tracks in the grass, just follow them and you'll be on a road that'll take you up past the landslide and then to fourteen. Fourteen goes to Fort Collins, so go then to I-25 and south to 70. Sound good?"

"Drive on the grass?"

"Yeah, everyone does it. Ain't gonna be a ramp there ever so we all just made our own."

"Thank you, Ron D., for the coffee, the company, and the directions. I owe you, man."

"Hey, ain't nothing."

In the fifteen foot walk from the door to Colander my hair gets wetter, the paper bulges with water spots. In the Volare, my shoulders and back are cold and drip down the seat. I set my coffees on the passenger's seat, start my car and check the gas, plenty. Dawn begins and while there is no sun, the clouds and night, just half an hour ago so dark, have begun to turn a faint blueish-gray; the area looks as if it is immersed. The rain is harder now but I follow the road up to the bridge and surely enough there's a series of paths in the dirt.

The paths are inclines of varying steepness. Some my car could not take in dry weather. There is one, though, which is gentle enough to take Colander onto the road. It will put us facing the wrong direction, but a U-turn fixes that. I sit in the rain mentally driving the path over and over until I can see the exact course, where my tires will go, and when I will steer. I drink one of my coffees and hold the other as we creep down the incline. The dirt is mud and the mud is slick. I hold my brakes on and my car slides until

136

enough grass and mud chock in front of the tires that we stop. I back up some and drive over the bumps and keep going, sliding onto the road. Rain intensifies. The road ahead is a haze of water and splashes and my wipers clear my vision only for a half second. Though they're on high already, I try them again to see if they won't go higher.

Colander fishtails some, but comes back in line. He is a good car like that, easy to control, dependable, consistent. I keep sipping coffee and periodically glance at the newspaper photo. Lightning moves in veins through the clouds and shows deep, rippled pools next to the road, on the road, across the road. I drive cautiously through the necessary ones, sure not to stall my car, hoping to avoid potholes or hidden dips. There is enough lightning that the man on the radio can't complete a sentence without a shadow of static. Thunder combs his words.

Dawn lightens the clouds' blue. The rain has not lessened any, but I allow myself to speed because there are no cars and The Universe is protecting me. To the left of the road is a cliff downward into a brown river. It churns and whirlpools. Trees are pitched in it like boats or soap in a child's bath. After a time driving, and long after the coffees are gone, nature calls. I pull to the side and turn on my blinkers, just in case, walk to the cliff's guardrail and unzip my fly. My shirt, hair, shorts, everything soaks in the rain. Water streams down my face and becomes waterfalls off my forehead and nose. The river is full up. It is filled with rapids no sane man would brave. The sound overpowers the rain, but not the thunder. I pull my penis out and as soon as a raindrop hits it a warm stream of yellow urine shoots out and into the canyon. I watch it quickly camouflaging itself with the rain as it falls the forty-or-so feet to the river below.

The far slope of a mountain, the canyon's other side, is perhaps a half-mile off and shrouded behind heavy rain and the sky's obscuring light. The canyon's river destroys itself in the throes of madness, the fits of delirium tremens.

I roll a section of my scrotum between my fingers because it itches but, overall, everything feels good, is charged with little, thunderless lightning bolts because I'm invincible, protected, peeing off a cliff, and all nature can see that I've got myself out for the world to look at and isn't it magnificent!

‹◊›

I eat a granola bar from my glove box for lunch as I drive. I have stopped often this morning, finishing most of my film. I photograph the plants, river alongside the road, the deepening water filling it and brown that churn like anger, rain drops splashing on cupped plant leaves, and Colander, alongside the road. He is a good car, and handsome.

In places there are trees with hockey-stick trunks, moss that hangs on the walls like a giant green perm, and thick roots that protrude out and down, around and back in. Above the sheerness of the canyon is a forest of pines. Not the sort of manicured, conical pines sold for Christmas trees, but tall, thick-trunked pines with scraggly branches and missing chunks. I drive slowly to take it in.

High beams appear in my periphery, around a turn and in my lane, moving fast. A horn blares and behind the lights a brown Cadillac comes toward me. The driver's highs turn off and his arms move the wheel. His eyes are wide; his face is terror and I know now that I am not invincible and am a small, useless, perfectly replaceable sprocket who is about to die.

The brown Caddy's rear end begins to slip and the whole car turns sideways. Everything slows as it hits Colander's front end. The air baffles below my bumper crumble, fender and hood bulge in and up. Glass from the Cadillac's driver's window slides over Colander's hood. He was moving too fast, no question. I was in my lane, well under the speed limit. The Volare, grabbed by the swinging momentum of the other car, is pushed sharply back and to the left and my head hits the passenger headrest. The world goes starry but they blink off, and the horizontal canyon layers are vertical. A piece of guardrail falls with me. In the other car the man stares at me through his broken window and I can hear him scream through my shut window, or maybe I hear myself scream; he holds his arm.

My car yaws hard when it hits the water. His car rolls upside-down. At the seams around my doors, water comes in. The Cadillac sinks in a bouquet of bubbles. The Volare hits it and rocks up, over, and is pushed backwards by the river. The floor of Colander takes on a thin brown broth which deepens as we sink. It smells like fish and biomass and the inside of Michael's Airstream. Water creeps up the front of the car and the grill sinks, Colander's engine stops.

I undo my seatbelt but the water is already over the window. It streams in through the edges along the window, the doors, a small branch lodges in the louvers of the rear window. The car grows dark as what little light the day provided is cut off. When I turn the dome light on, the river's true nature shows itself. Gravel, sand, and rocks are carried by my window. The ping off my car like the hail in Saint Louis.

I will never see my parents again.

They will never know what happened.

My body probably won't be found.

My car may never be found.

Rick and my other friends, like Amy, will wonder what happened and why I ran away. No one will ever know what I did and learned out here. I will be a face on a milk carton, or a flier on a light pole, or a postcard advertising a muffler shop or ambulance-chasing lawyer on the other side.

I touch the window. It is cold. "I guess you're not taking care of me after all," I say to The Universe.

My parents will no longer have to stay married, at least.

The water first shows its coldness when it covers my shoes and hits my ankles. Outside the river grows a darker brown, nearing black, grittier, and larger pieces of rock and debris stream past, loud when they hit. One rock hits the driver's side window and it cracks, a dollar-bill length crack running up the middle of the glass. But it holds and no water seeps through.

When the water hits my crotch I feel my pants grow warm and the heat of my urine against the cold of the water is like the flipping of a switch in my brain. This is not how nor where I want to be buried. There must be something to save myself with.

The seats won't float, nor will I. The back seat reminds me of the camera case. It's water tight; it will float. It has a handle. I pull my keys from the ignition. Climbing into the backseat is like climbing a slide, the car has listed that far forward. With my Swiss Army knife I cut an "I" into the vinyl of the backseat. It peels away and the dark yellow foam padding tears in chunks. When I get to the particle board, I press against the driver's seat and kick the bare wood. The water is up to my ribs and my teeth chatter as much from the cold as knowing I won't ever get to apologize for running away. The overhead light is my only light and it shows everything outside is black. We are completely submerged and my only hope is that my trunk is at least mostly dry. My foot breaks through the board and water flows in.

There is no hope, no camera case, it seems, until the water stops and I can see that the camera rests on the other side of the particle board. A large something hits my car, pushing it upright and I hold the particle board, the water in the vertical cabin around my waist. We roll upside-down.

Colander is dark, but the dome light is still on under the water, turning the floor of the car a strange vomit-brown-burgundy color with dancing dark lines across it. I focus and pull on the particle board, break away pieces of it which float in the water next to the foam, newspaper and empty coffee cups. I reach the camera case and pull it through. I hug it quickly. "Thank you, Colander, for having a stuck trunk."

I undo the locks fast, the case floats on the rising water. In the case I set my wallet, glasses, sunglasses, keys, and dripping journal. I close the case, lock it, and wait for the water to fill the car. When the water reaches the window cranks the dome light begins to flicker and then goes out. I hear myself crying out to a God I haven't talked to in three years, begging Him for a second chance, apologizing for my arrogance, pleading for His help. In the blackness I sit, clutching my case with both hands, my nose to the floor, waiting, praying.

And then it happens: I take my last breath before the car is all water; my mouth tastes of dirt and sand. I use my camera case, the internal air pulling it to the floor, as a hammer against the driver's window. Pulling it down to the window is hard and I feel my lungs convulse, looking for air. The glass breaks easily, or perhaps I slam the case hard into it, adrenaline and fear strengthening me more than years of lifting weights could. The case is nearly yanked from my hands by the current. I feel remnant shards cut across my arms, chest, back and legs and I am pulled violently from the car. The camera and the current fight over whether I will live or drown. The argument seems to take minutes, or hours. I know from Boy Scouts I could once hold my breath for three minutes and seventeen seconds. But that's three minutes and seventeen seconds at rest in warm water. Under cold water, afraid of drowning, eyes closed, any sense of space lost, my time could be less than a half minute. My lungs spasm, push out and pull in, looking for air, little blasts of exhale purse my lips and water trickles in, sand gets between my teeth. It would be easy to drink in the drowning mud, or let go of the camera, and drowning doesn't seem so bad right now. There would be no burning in my lungs, no panic as water filled my nose and throat. It would be peaceful, relaxing, a culmination of where I am to be at this confluence of time, the end result of the last three weeks deposition of me, here, in this river. I would be the salmon and I would know the fullness of it all, inhaling nature's rage, understanding my reason for being was solely to be here, at this place, to cash in the karmic retribution of my arrogance.

No. Drowning would suck. I would never see daylight, never feel the chill of inhaled winter air, sweat in hot sunlight. Panic hits. The camera case could be stuck under some submerged log and we may not be ascending after all. The current may be too tumultuous and my added weight too much for us to surface. I force myself to focus on hoping one thing: that the camera case pulls me toward air. Debris hits my body, sometimes with a considerable amount of force, putting flashing lights on my eyelids and knocking the last air from my lungs.

As I begin to pray again the case wins. It breaks the surface and pulls me out as well. I breathe in wet air and mud and hold on to the case. My lungs burn, still shake from the absence of air they haven't realized is past. I keep my right hand on the handle and clear silty water from my face with my left. The river splashes over me, breaks on rocks, whirlpools in places. I see no debris from my car. Colander is upside-down, submerged. Perhaps he hopes I am alive, hopes his keeping the trunk shut saved me. He put my life above his own. Why?

I look for the other driver but don't see him. I hold on to my case and look at the canyon, fifty feet high or more here, on both sides; its narrowness bucking and breaking around me and I wish whoever has the cord around this rivers' balls would let go.

I yell it, and yell, yell it until my jaw hurts from yelling and screaming and I can't even talk. All I can do is grip the black, industrial plastic case with both hands and hope that at some point this river has banks. I feel my legs hit rocks and trees underwater and my shoes get pulled off, one at a time. Then my socks fill with wet, viscous silt and fall off my feet, too. I squeeze my legs and push out what little gut I have in hopes of keeping my shorts. The weight I have lost these weeks works against me. Mud builds in my underwear. It is cold and moves up through the legs of my shorts into my jockeys and stays there, building.

Left of me are two rows of submerged train cars. The tops of them show above the water, mounds of evenly piled coal rest on them. They are safety. Down river is a bridge and the cars go under it. I could swim to the cars, climb onto them, and then sit at the bridge waiting for help. I kick toward the cars but the current pulls me away. Two police squads with flashing lights drive over the bridge. The train cars move further away from me and soon I am under the bridge and past the saving mounds of coal.

The river looks like conching chocolate. Frothing, white crested waves splash over me and ahead I see a whirlpool with a spinning, near-vertical telephone pole. I kick away, hoping that will help. Above the sound of the rapids, above the rain hitting the canyon and the river, I frantically ask God for help, again. And maybe this has been going on all along, but it surprises me to learn it now. Something saves me, though, the kicking or God (not The Universe), because I miss the telephone pole and the whirlpool.

Hoping for some kind of miracle or Divine intervention, I keep looking around for the other driver, or a sign of his car, "Are you out there? Are you okay?" The river boffs at me. There is no time in this canyon, with this sky. No noon, no AM or PM, no sunset, no dusk, no evening, just a simple, ever-present sullen grayness. Only when the canyon turns indigo and the water black does it seem any more like evening. In time, seeing no beaches or people or the other driver, I give up and just hold on to the camera case and wait for an eventual widening of the river and hope there isn't a waterfall anywhere. Debris hits my feet and shins, sometimes it hurts enough I expect to pass out or inadvertently let go of the case. The roof of a house, inverted, still largely intact, floats past. A dog is on it, wet and barking. I am too tired to swim to it.

‹0›

When the river widens, the rapids calm and end. The air and water have chilled; my teeth click out a morse code of coldness. Things stop hitting my body and a throbbing sets in all over: in my arms from holding the case, my chest from the case's movements in the river, torso and legs from debris. Every inch of skin registers heartbeats. I begin counting them to stay awake. The river is calm and I want to just float and sleep, but then the river would win. The river will not win. I can do this shit. Time still does not truly exist, but the clouds above take their time clearing, and the parade shines on. They remind me of my utter sprocketness and replaceability.

When a shore does appear it is a crescent of moonlight in the shadow of trees. I kick to it and crawl across its round, fist-sized stones. I set the case level and undo the combination locks. They grind as I turn their faces, thin drops of muddy water, black in the pale-indigo moonlight, trickle from inside them. I open the case expecting the inside to be an umber soaking of the foam rubber padding. But instead I find it dry, except around the journal. The camera, the lenses, are as if nothing had happened. My glasses are unhurt and I put them on, close the case and lock it, walk up the shore, hunched low from an impact to my gut, slowly to not slip on the algal rocks, and when I reach grass I set the case down and sit on it.

Stars, meteoric flashes, and a satellite span the zenith. Some of the stars that made those lights may not exist anymore, but at this moment they do. It's odd: They may have died thousands or millions of years ago, but their effect is seen still. Perhaps that is what life calls us to aspire to.

These three weeks haven't happened for nothing. Not to say they were destined, or that at this specific time I could not have possibly been anywhere else except sitting on my camera case watching the sky over a black river, cold and alone under the stars. No, but at some point in my life I would have been here. Here. This river bank the ultimate product of managing to somehow float down this conch of mixing mud, saved by the air-, dust-, and water-tight case that my parents told me was a waste of money, being twenty-four hours early for the Antelope Canyon flood, being picked up and driven when I ran out of gas, not falling down the Grand Canyon, not passing out there; being called to Colorado by my grandfather's grave.

I take off my shirt and shorts and lie on the thick, well-tended grass, curled as tightly as possible on my right side, calming as the bodily throbbing slows, listening to the river's adagio tenor, waiting to sleep.

‹◊›

Bird songs and warm sunlight wake me. I wipe the crust of sleep off my eyes, feel it crumble and bounce off the bridge of my nose. I take my glasses from the ground and put them on. My legs are columns of bruise. My feet are coated in a dry layer of muck, it cracks and breaks off as I wiggle my toes. My feet are lumpy and two toenails on my right foot are gone. Cuts cross-stitch my feet, shins and thighs – line my arms, chest, and shoulders like hatch marks counting off interred days. Most cuts are crusted over by blood and mud. Some on my feet re-open when I peel muck off. My stomach is bruised in a perfect, plate-sized circle. All things considered, I got out of the river pretty well off. I stand, flex my arms in front of me, showing the river it lost, but when I stretch my abdomen it clenches in pain, and I fall on the rocks, resting there a time. The river here is calm, no way resembling the torrent last night.

I dress in my once white now earthen and torn shirt and shorts. The slices in them line up with the cuts to my arms and chest. Some along my stomach are deep and should have had stitches; they will heal and scar and in time the scars will fade. Amy once told me that fading scars are a sad thing. Scars are souvenirs. They remind, when we're thirty, or fifty, until they fade, that all the events of our lives actually happened. I stumble and look at my arms, paler than they were yesterday though the tan has not faded. My jockeys are filled with mud and silt and take some scooping clean. Putting on my shorts hurts; lifting my legs hurts. By the time I have dressed my body again throbs my pulse.

Around me is a throstle of weeds and pine trees. I am on the gentle hill overlooking the still, vicious river. The body of a drowned cow floats by. Carrying my camera case, I walk up the hill, pine needles pricking into my feet like a thousand shots. No level of endorphins can chink this pain. At the top of the small hill I look out and see a truck stop with a mini-mart, a gas station, a twenty-four-hour diner, two fast-food restaurants, some small, old houses, and a less descript brick building with a tall radio tower behind it.

145

There are three police cars parked in front of it. I walk in that building's direction.

Around the trees the air smells clean, decisive, vanilla. Birds in the pine trees chirp, perhaps to see who weathered the storm and who did not. On a length of grass before the police station, the air is warmer, humid. The sun reminds me it is there. It seems to want to tell me it has not finished with me, but it has. I will not go against it again; nature is a lover who has hurt me, has apologized by placing me here. Maybe she will not hurt me again. Bird sounds dissipate, replaced by the radio antenna's thrumming; the air is static and dead.

The parking lot's pavement is cool. The door opens and inside the world becomes cold, canned. The sound of birds, replaced by the antenna, is now one of a ringing phone, shuffling papers, two people talking, a can of pop opening, and the air conditioning moving through the ventilation. All but the ringing phone and moving air stop when the door chimes my entrance. Police officers look at me and I begin to think about how I must look to others. The columns of pain that are my legs give way and I fall to the hard, cold tile floor.

I am on a bed in a jail cell. My muddy clothes have been replaced by clean jail fatigues. The door to the cell is open, though. My feet have been cleaned and dressed and my ankles and knees are wrapped in athletic bandages. I sit upright, against the soreness of my legs, feeling the circular platter of pain on my stomach. My legs burn, throb in time with my heart beat; the throbbing and pain quicken as I walk stiffly from the cell.

There are three people in a large jail cell. One looks hung over, one reads, one does pushups and, when he sees me, runs to the front of his cell.

"I don't know how you got out, but you gotta let me out. I'm fucking dying in here. This cell's gonna kill me."

He looks to be moving back and forth, but I know it's not him. The bars and the cell and the whole station are in flux. Or maybe it's just me. "Where am I?"

"Pine Grove Stand police station, buddy. Go get the keys for me. Come on, man." His voice sounds as if he stands on the precipice of tears.

My legs and feet are beyond throbbing with my pulse, beyond the acute burning of the lacerations. This pain is on a new plane of existence and there are not words for it: no one has ever had to explain it before. "This town has three words in its name? That's gotta be hard to get used to." I walk to the front of the cell block, to a door, and knock on it. It opens in a minute and there stands a female officer taller than I. Mammoth breasts are evident through her bullet-proof vest. She puts a hand on my shoulder and walks me into the station. The tiles are cold under my feet and the air, the dead stir, wraps my skin in gooseflesh.

"Where's my clothes?"

"Your suitcase is in lockup for you. Your clothes were torn to pieces and we threw them out. A couple guys went out to the local K-Mart to get you a couple new sets. We figured you'd not wake up till today, so we didn't bother doing it when you got in."

"That could be the nicest thing anyone has done for me in a long time."

She smiles as she helps me sit in a comfortable, cloth chair. She sits in a desk next to me. "Do you know where you are?"

"The guy who wants let out said I'm in Grove Stand Pines."

"Close enough."

"Where is that?"

"About thirty miles from Utah."

"How'd I get like this?"

"Like what?"

"Clean, bandaged, in these clothes."

"You walked into the station at three sixteen yesterday afternoon," she said. The little hand of a clock on her desk points almost to the one and the big hand to the eleven. "You proceeded to pass out. So we had the town doctor check you out. Nearest hospital is over three hours away and Doc Ponzo said you'd be fine without a trip, just needed sleep and some butterfly stitches." She points to my abdomen. "No broken bones, a few bruised maybe, but nothing serious. Lots of bruising in your legs; lacerations to your arms, legs, chest and back; two serious cuts on your gut. Both should have had stitches, but he cleaned them and put on the butterflies, best he could do. Said you musta lost some blood, too. You're pale."

"I feel weak."

"There's a big bruise on your abdomen, too. Overall, though, nothing that won't be fully healed in a few weeks. But you gotta take it easy."

A few weeks. That should be sometime after school starts. I imagine meeting my roommate for the first time, my legs green and brown, pink lines of infant scars. I talked to him on the phone, once, in July. He sounded nice enough. From not too far away from me, forty minutes west of Chicago. How would I explain the bruises? What would he think? He would sit in one of the dorm's wooden desk chairs, or on his desk, and ask me what I did. When he hears the story he thinks I am insane and says I shouldn't wear shorts until it's all healed. The bruises make him feel sick.

July, my parents, both so foreign. It is not as if I never lived everything else I have gone through, but it has all become a film that plays back at variable speeds, snowy and distorted, with similar outcomes. The past has become intangible as a photo. Once, I thought photos jogged memories, made places alive again.

"Now, tell me," she says, taking a pad and pen from a desk drawer, "how you got here."

In the corner of the office are two pizzas and a half-full bottle of pop. "Can I have some pizza and pop?" I ask.

She stands and brings me one of the pizza boxes, a half-eaten sausage and mushroom, and the two-liter of pop.

"It's all room-temp."

"That's okay," I say. "I forget when I ate last."

"So tell me how you got here. Let's start with you name."

"What today's date?"

"August seventeenth. We need to get some info about you, though."

"Merak Christopher Snyder." I look at the pizza, forgetting how to eat. Remembering, I pick up a slice and bite into it. The pizza has a dead, flat, vile sort of goodness. The sausage is crumbly and spicy and the mushrooms chewy and wet, but it tastes better than anything – ever. It has a newness, a texture and flavor unlike food has had before and perhaps it's not the taste of the food but the idea that I'm actually alive to taste it which fills my mouth and body with frisson. "In July I saw my mom with another man at the mall," I begin, telling the story through chewed crust. I tell her about how I avoided my parents and when I confronted my father, how he reacted. Then I tell her I ran away the next day. She motions for another officer.

"He's a runaway." She writes my name on a sheet of paper. "Could you look into it? Thanks, Scott."

I tell her about the Grand Canyon and Anna; about Watersharer; Michael and his father; Kimberly and the bear and salmon; my grandparents' markers and the cemetery's view of the town; the frogs and the accident, escaping my car and floating down that mud river; the shore of the river and walking over the hill to the police station. In the time I take telling her, I eat the pizza I was given and three slices of the other, a pepperoni and pepper thin crust. I drink the pop and five glasses of water. By the time I finish the story, officers have gathered to hear it. They ask questions about my camera case and how to get one, about the man in the Cadillac, and about Kimberly, especially. One of them gives a light nudge with his elbow, stopping when I wince. Scott sets a folder on the female officer's desk and walks away. He returns carrying new clothes, jeans with mis-stitched inseams, a Colorado Rockies shirt with misaligned print, and off-brand sneakers. Somehow they're the best looking clothes in existence. I thank the officers graciously.

The officers disperse, some rub the top of my head like they would a child, others shake my hand, one just shakes his head in disbelief and says "Damn, boy."

Scott sits opposite me, looking at the female officer. "He's been missing from Deer Lake, Illinois, for nearly three weeks. The local cops are on their way to contact the parents."

The parents. The words sound lost coming from someone else. Not so much from a different language, more like words which have been allowed to die and now, these Lazarus words, reanimated, ugly, necromantic and ghoulish, stumble awkwardly and search for footing in a place where they have been over-spoken and reached obsolescence.

"They're probably worried, Merak. They listed you as missing as soon as legally possible."

"I left them a note. Told them I'd call when I got settled."

"You'll understand when you have kids," says Scott. "They'll want to talk to you."

"Can we go get my car, first? They'll both be out so it'll be hours before they can talk to me, anyway." It takes some begging, telling them I'm not ready to talk to my parents, but the female officer, Rachel she says her name is when I remember to ask, finally agrees to drive me to where my car would be to see if it's retrievable. I change into my new clothes. They're a little tight, but fit fairly well. The jeans put a slight, cast-like pressure on my legs.

On the way out of town I see a dark brown, early eighties Nissan Sentra under a tree. It has a sign in the window "FOR SALE BY OWNER: $695 OBO"

We drive out the interstate and get off the exit where I did. It is a two-and-a-half hour drive at a quick clip with one bathroom stop.

"Is 70 opened yet?"

"Nope. Won't be for a while, I imagine. Two days or more. The dam break and the landslide have been too much for emergency crews to handle. It'll be a while clearing it all."

We drive down the grass and along the canyon. Past where I went to the bathroom, past the corners and turns until we see a broken section of guardrail. Rain drizzles. The squad car's wiper blades whirr and squeak when they move. I step out of the car. A ghost image of the Cadillac slides. The driver counter-steers and heads toward me. Colander passes through me from behind, the brake lights on, me turning the steering wheel. The faint forms of the cars hit and my car bucks hard left with the impact, throwing my head into the passenger's headrest. The ghosts pass through me and the other driver's knuckles are white as he holds his arm, face contorted into a scream. The Cadillac's engine whines a loose belt whine. It is the serpentine belt. It once went on the Volare.

Rachel walks to the edge and looks down. "Water's still too deep to see much."

I look over the edge. Somewhere down there is my car. "How deep do you think it is?"

Rachel looks at the far side, at the top of a submerged train engine. "It's at least fifteen feet right now. Your car could be miles downstream. Odds are it'll never be recovered, or if so then not for months. And even then, I hope you weren't too attached to it because it's not going to ever be drivable again."

"Oh." I had, until now, imagined it would be towed back but, with some cleaning and a new back seat, be just fine. My father had been planning the Volare as his next project car.

We get back in the police car, our hair shines with gem-drops of water. She turns the heat on and we drive back to the police station. When we get there Scott greets us. "That was nearly six hours, Rachel. His parents want him to call them at home."

‹◊›

Rachel and Scott give me a private office to use. It's empty except for a desk and a phone. The carpet and wallpaper are circa-1974 dark beige. The wall has a level surround of light squares where pictures or plaques had hung, a bookshelf had stood. Rachel explains that the detective who had it retired and the vacancy has yet to be filled, doesn't really need to be. She picks up the phone and types in her long distance code. "You have thirty seconds to begin typing the number." She hands me the receiver and leaves, shutting the door tight behind her. The office would be a sad picture, empty.

The dial tone sounds in my ear like an anxious, crying child. I push the 1-708 and forget my own phone number. But I remember it, number at a time, like a book read as a child which, when read ten years later, re-reveals each subsequent chapter as the previous ends. It rings once before my mother picks up.

"Hello?" Her voice cracks. The line clicks. "Hello?" It is my father.

"Hi, Mom, Dad."

"Merak, oh Good Lord, you're all right," cries Mother. I hear her knees thump onto the floor. Her voice resonates, she is in the master bathroom, in all likelihood lying on the floor. I hear her cry. "Are you okay?"

"I am." I lie down on the desk to take the pressure off my legs.

"Good, boy." My father's talking. "Now you listen up. You had us and your friends scared shitless. Do you understand that? Amy's been here asking for updates when she could. Rick calls incessantly. They've been out

152

taping fliers with your picture to telephone poles, combing the fields and forests with the police. Your face has been all over the news out here. Did you even think about what you might do to us? Do you know how selfish this was? Do you even think before you act?"

"Richard –"

"Not now, Margret. Merak, you get your ass home A-S-A-P. Do you understand. You get to an airport and you fly home today. I'll find a way to get your car back here after school starts. You have a lot to answer for."

His voice has as much envy as anger. What is so special about this ability to pick up and leave, the decision to, that Anna, Michael, and now my own father find appealing. Returning will not be the quiet, unnoticed event I had imagined.

"Why? Why do I want to come home. Especially since you're pissed. You two have lied my whole life about yourselves. And what if I don't, are you just not going to talk to me for six years, Dad?"

The line is quiet dead air. Using my biggest gun, tipping my hand to show that I can deal back just as much pain as they've handed me, this early was a mistake. I breathe through my nose, calm myself, but feel my pulse quicken. The second-hand on the lobby wall clock passes five lines before he speaks.

"Why'd you tell him about that, Margaret?"

"I didn't tell him. You must have."

"Do you think I'd tell him that?"

"Yes. Then you'd forget it and blame it on me. That'd be just like you and your constant revisions of history."

"Who revises history? Not me, missy. You're the one who can't keep a story straight from telling to telling."

"Grandpa told me. Before he died. In a letter."

"Oh," says my mother. "That should surprise me less than it does."

"He did?"

"Yes, Dad."

"I didn't know that." My father feels betrayed, like a convict promised an appeal that turns out to be a death sentence. Something in his voice tells me that this was bigger than the six-years comment. I may never know why we hurt each other, but I've been instructed well in the doing of it.

"Merak, honey, look. Sometimes people fall in and out of love with each other. And the times your father and I don't love each other just happen to occur opposite each other's. But you should come home. We still love you."

"Margret, you haven't ever loved me."

"Do you believe that?"

"Mom – Dad"

"Of course I do, Margret. What else should I believe? You never did anything to show it. Never once said it to me."

"It's the man's job to say it first, and I don't not love you."

"That's horseshit. Horseshit, Margaret. And you know it. All of it is horseshit."

"Dad, Mom, can you stop?"

"When have you ever loved me?"

"You're a good father, Richard."

"But you don't love me. Loving me as a father isn't loving me it's loving one aspect of me –"

"What are you talking about?"

" – and that isn't love, that's affection, or puppy love, or a crush at best. It's abusive, Margaret. You're being abusive."

"I'm being abusive?"

"We'd never have married if you didn't trap me with pregnancy. This is exactly why."

"Good Christ, you two."

"This is not something we need to discuss now." Her voice is calm, but bitter. The monotone steadiness of it tells me that no matter how bad things get on the phone, the real argument will come later.

"Then when? We've not discussed it for almost twenty years."

"You are so the woman in this marriage, Richard."

Sharp, cracking sounds pour across the line and into the office. Mom sighs. "That did it." Seconds later Father picks up again.

"See what you made me do? You made me break the goddamned phone, Margaret."

"I didn't make you do anything, Richard. You did it on your own."

"Oh, yes, and you'd know what doing something on your own means, too. You'd recognize your behavior."

"What does that even mean?"

"Can you stop fighting for just a minute?"

"It means Brian and all the others."

"Oh, aren't you so the wounded male, Richard. Oh, my pain, my pain, pity me, pity me. I've been hurt. Lick your injuries later, we're not going into this right now."

"Why not now? He knows. It's your fault. You were meandering around the mall, his hangout, like a goddamned floozy. You wanted him to find out."

"That's not fair." Her voice cracks and shakes. She sniffles. It is far from the first time Father's words have made her cry.

"Truth isn't always fair. You wanted him to find out so I wouldn't have to tell him. You were afraid if I told him then he'd run away, but AH-HA! Hoisted by your own petard, woman."

"No. No it isn't. It was his day off. It doesn't matter. Why are you doing this in front of Merak?"

"He needs to hear it, Margaret. It's his future now—"

"Stop it, please," I plead.

"—thanks to you."

"Not thanks to me," Mother says

"Good move, good move indeed," father says

"You did a bad job in the telling, Dad."

Mother's sobs come through the phone line, Father's breaths do, too. They are like music, a slow background of sobbing with a loud foreground of furious respiration.

"Did you ever think about the approach you could take? You had eighteen years to figure out a better way to tell me than your dad did, and he didn't even do a bad job. No, instead you spent eighteen years trying to figure out how to pass your made up trauma and anger onto me. Grandpa at least loved Grandma and they would have gotten married anyway. You have to spend your time rubbing everyone's' faces in just how much Mom hates you and you hate her, and what a bad marriage you have, and why everyone should feel so bad for you. I'm done with it. I'm leaving your pity party behind. You made your bed and you need to sleep quietly from here out."

One of the phones on the other end of the line is set down and I hear the garage door open and his Saab start. It backs out of the garage.

"Great, just what he needs to be doing when he's this mad – driving."

"He'll be okay, Mom. I'm sorry he said all that stuff."

"It's alright. What have you been up to for almost three weeks? It's been a long three weeks here."

"I know it has, now." I tell Mom the whole story like I told Grandfather. I begin in Saint Louis with how there's not a lot to see in

Illinois, but even if there were, Interstate travel is too fast to get a good look at it. She listens intently as I tell her everything Grandfather wrote me about meeting Grandmother and the trail and where they went, how it's still just like that.

"I'd never heard that story. I didn't know any of it."

She likes Watersharer, is even jealous for her freedom to go and do and be her own boss and the solitude of it all. I tell her about Antelope Canyon and its ethereal beauty, and leave the rest of that day behind, like the newspaper I left behind in Colander. The shortest section is the visit to Grandfather because I figure she doesn't want to hear about it. I tell her about the view of the town, the church, the absolute quiet of the mountainside. I tell her that I should have been able to go and she agrees, and apologizes. Apologies are nice to have, but they don't change the past.

I am about to tell her about losing the Volare and floating in the river when the Saab pulls back into the garage. The clock on the lobby wall says I have been on the phone almost an hour and a half.

Father picks the receiver back up. "I realized what it is, Merak. I know this whole freedom thing, and I'm willing to let your insolence slide for right now because you're out there, you think you have it all figured out, that you're some kind of loner-philosopher, some kind of hardcore badass. But you'll see differently when you get back."

"I realized what it is, too. You're jealous."

"What do you have that I'd be jealous of?"

I tap the side of the phone in time with the beat of my heart, which is well over a hundred.

"Well?"

"This is so childish, Richard."

It's not what I have, Father, instead what I don't have — self-hatred, hate for my life. I don't want the world to feel bad for me. When I'm not happy with something I change it instead of whining. That's what makes you jealous, is what I want to say. "What are you going to do, Dad, spank me? There's no punishment you can levy that will ever have any effect."

His teeth grind and I know he wants to say something, wants to find some words to use to bring me to my knees. He may have them in his arsenal, but if he does he chooses not to use them. "They say you're in Colorado. Stand Pine Grove, or something. When will you be home?"

"I don't know. Depends on when I can get a car."

"What happened to the Volare. No, better, just start at the beginning." My father's voice is one of calm authority, and simultaneously the opposite, exactly like all the times he went from angry to pleasant in just seconds. When he would try to fix a problem with the Ferrari and make another by kicking it, or throwing a piece of the engine into the side or floor of the garage and how he would then breathe deeply, think rationally, and go replace whatever part he had just broken. Or how once when a stray dog had me cornered, looked ready to attack, he tackled it, hitting it and fighting with it, somehow avoiding bites and serious scratches, and managed to tighten its choke collar enough to make it pass out.

I don't want to tell them the story, having just told it, but someone needs to speak. I begin with Anna, but do not tell them the truth of it: That I wanted to stay in Arizona and fix Anna's problems, give her the kind of life I have had. I expect him to ask me if I did her, or something, but he doesn't and I suppose that's because those sort of conversations between a father and son are not meant for a mother's ears. In time I get to the part about the rain storm and the Cadillac and how my car got knocked into the river. Mother gasps and asks how I got out. I tell her and Father laughs, and says "that's my boy!" He'd pat me on the back and give me a beer, were he in the same room.

"Merak, it's very important for you to understand that I still love your father, and part of him loves me, too."

"Not this again," I say.

"Don't lie to him." "I'm not."

"Stop fighting."

"I do love you." "When?"

"When I see you with him. When you do things together. When you talk about work and cars, Richard. The same things that attracted me to you in the beginning. You're right, though. I shouldn't lie to him because I know you don't love me anymore."

"How can you say you love me? You had the first affair – the first two – and didn't tell me till I found out years later."

"What else was I supposed to do? We haven't had sex since our honeymoon."

"Can't you talk about this when I'm not listening?

"Well you didn't want it."

"I was pregnant! And it was a bad pregnancy, too. Don't act like you don't remember. You held my hair back while I was at the toilet each morning. You were the one running out for ginger ale at two a.m. because my stomach was upset. You held the cold compresses to my forehead when I sweated so bad the mattress drowned."

"Well, yeah."

"So don't give me that crap about not loving me."

"I didn't say it – you did. You did with Dennis and Mark. Mark was my best man, for Christ's sake, Margaret. You said it with Lou and Frank, now Brian."

"Oh, oh, me is it, it's always me. What about Christine?"

"Who?"

"That chunky red head you were sleeping with after you got me pregnant."

"That stopped when you told me you were pregnant."

I rub my forehead. My brain presses against it, tries like a felon to escape.

"I would have told you sooner if you hadn't been fucking her. Did you think I'd not find out? She lived four doors down from me, Richard."

"Well, I knew you'd find out. But we both agreed it was just physical and not exclusive."

"You agreed to that."

"Hey," I say.

"What did you see in her? You always said I was more fun to be around. You enjoyed our time together. You actually stayed the night with me, once in a while."

"We really don't need to discuss this."

"What did you see in her?

"Margaret, really, don't do this to yourself, or Merak."

"You leave Merak out of this. What did you see in her?"

"She did this . . . thing."

" 'Thing?' "

"This thing."

"I really don't need to hear this," I say.

"What 'thing?' "

"I don't really think I want to explain with Merak listening."

"You two have had three weeks to have this discussion without me. And you have to wait until I'm around to do it?"

"What thing did she do?"

"We'll discuss it later. Besides, it was only her and Stephanie. And Steph ended a long time ago."

Mother pauses. "Steph. Yeah, I remember. All you ever talked about was Steph this, Steph that."

"Hey, I would have hung up–"

"Well, I mean, I loved her."

"–except that I need a thousand dollars."

"Loved her? Do you think of her still?"

"What did you say, Merak?" asks my father. "She's why we didn't move from Chicago, so yes I do still think about her. Every summer, Margaret, when it's humid," he added.

"I need a thousand dollars."

"What on earth do you need a thousand dollars for?"

"My car is under fifteen feet of river. There's a car here for sale and I need to buy one."

"The car is a thousand dollars? And no. Where am I supposed to get a thousand dollars from? You're getting on a bus and going to an airport."

"It's like seven hundred for the car. It'd be cheaper than me flying home. And no busses are going to Denver because I-70 is closed. But I need gas money and it may need some repairs, or something." I open my wallet, it has just over two hundred dollars left in it.

"You're west of Denver? How far west?"

"Utah, basically."

"How's a car going to help you if the roads are closed, Merak?" says my mother.

"I know a way around the closure. If you want, I'll just get the car and abandon it at the Denver airport. I don't care."

"No. You're getting on a bus–"

"There are no fucking busses." My vacation is not ending with me on a bus.

161

He pauses. "I see. I still don't have a thousand dollars for you to buy a car with."

"But you have more than that for me to fly home with. Your savings account has fifty-two hundred dollars and change in it. Don't leave bank statements on the counter."

"Is there a Western Union or something out there?" Mom asks.

"Should be. I saw a currency exchange. Look, I'm on someone else's dime. I'm going to hang up. I'll check the currency exchange in an hour or so to get the money and the town name is Pine Grove Stand. P-G-S, remember it that way, or something. I don't care."

"Take care, honey," Mom says.

"Be careful out there, son," says my dad. "I love you."

"Love you, too." I say and hang up the phone. I press the receiver into the cradle, look at the empty desk and rest my weight on it, embracing the pressure from my jeans. When I leave the office Rachel says that I didn't do much talking, except twice. And I say that they mostly fought.

Rachel nods. She does not understand.

A woman pushing a stroller with twins walks into the police station. She looks at me and smiles, asks Rachel if Scott is around. When Scott arrives he greets her with a hug and a kiss on the lips. He picks one of the children, a toddler, from the stroller and carries him as his wife pushes the stroller to Scott's desk. There are three pictures of her and two of each of the children on it. They sit and talk quietly as Scott holds his son, who tries to climb on him and the desk. Scott raspberries his stomach. The child giggles and kicks.

"They've been married eleven years," says Rachel. "Doctors said it'd be impossible for them to have kids. Then they had little Scotty there. The miracle baby they called him. Still do. Their miracle son. Then a year and a half later come along baby Emma. Scott and Chris love those kids so much," says Rachel.

"I've been watching them less than three minutes and they've shown more intimacy than I can remember my parents showing."

"I'm sorry," she says.

"You're lucky it's something you can't understand."

"I am. You're going to be free to leave soon enough. You're eighteen. Not much we can do, like make you go home. It's one hundred percent your call."

"I will be. I have to go to college."

"To get your education?"

"And degree."

"Different things, you know," she says. "A degree just says you paid too many thousands of dollars for some paper. An education, that's wholly internal. No teacher can educate you."

"How so?"

"You'll see when you get there."

In an hour, Rachel puts my camera case in the backseat of her squad car. I shake the hands of Scott and the other officers. I offer to pay them back for the clothes but they say no, repeatedly, and in time I accept. The Universe, or more likely God, it seems, wants me to have my money. Rachel and I stop at the currency exchange for the thousand dollars then at the house with the car for sale. The man who is selling it is a tall, broad Mexican with the hands and body from years of physical labor. His hair is dark and face creviced. He has not had a happy life.

"I can give you five hundred for the car," I say, when he opens the door to his trailer.

"The price is seven hundred."

"I'll give you five hundred now, no questions asked."

"Seven."

"Think you'll get a better offer then five?"

He steps back and the door begins to shut.

"Six," I say.

"Six," he says, looking thoughtful. He rubs his chin. "I can part with it for six."

I take the money, all in fifties because I asked for it that way. "Fifty-one, fifty-two, fifty-three, fifty-four, fifty-five, fifty-six," I say, laying the bills out one at a time. He takes them and counts them. Satisfied, he folds the money and sticks it between his pants and skin. He lets the screen door shut but leaves the front door open. From a stack of sheets and envelopes on a kitchen table he pulls the title and hands it to me.

He takes the keys from a drawer, drops them into my hand, and says "drive safe, now."

The car is perfumed by burned hair, cigarettes, and crotch sweat. It starts without a problem. The radio has a tape deck and tunes easily. The absence of the ratcheting finalizes Colander's loss. Here is this new car, it could be loyal or it could be vindictive. It is not, in any way, Colander. It will not have the rumble of Colander's engine, the slight shake between fifty and sixty miles per hour, the body panels or the words "Road Runner" printed along the door bottom. It is not in any way reminiscent of serious cars.

The Nissan's radio station is set to Spanish music. After putting my camera in the trunk, next to the spare tire, jacks, and a very large box of expensive tools, I wave to Rachel, who pulls away from the car. In town I fill up the tank, clean the windows, buy some snacks and juice, pop, anything drinkable which is not water, and look out at the small town. I think about the people here, the road ahead, and behind, and how any single change in anything in my life would have me elsewhere at this moment. And elsewhere would not be as good as here.

7
Birch Naked

Pine Grove Stand is not twenty miles behind when a man walking the roadside turns, walks backwards, and puts his thumb out. He freezes, a picture of a lone man in a red cap, backpack, and faded jeans standing on a serpentine road in a semi-tunnel of trees. The day is cool, in the upper-seventies, overcast in a way which hides any sign of cardinal directions, but still bright enough that the road is darkened by the sepulcher-like pines on each side. Even on a sunny day this road would be shaded. The man jacks his arm back and forth at the elbow. Inside my head, a new voice, my voice as I wish it sounded, says, "do not stop."

Driving past, as I have always done with hitchhikers, is my first idea. However, I wouldn't be here if it weren't for strangers, so I slow and stop just past him. As he jogs I unlock the passengers' side doors. "Toss your stuff in the back." I had been listening to country music, to a peculiar desperation that accompanies some of the love songs, wondering why those songs felt more honest than modern pop rock. In the name of politeness, though, I turn off the radio and watch the antenna go partway down then get caught on and stop at the bend in it. I adjust how I sit, letting the blood flow in my legs change; the bruises pump against the jeans. My legs and back are tired of road time, stiff and sore, ready for my bed, or the couch in the living room, or maybe just the carpeting on the finished side of the basement. I want to simply drive, no stops, no sleep, get home and face the future. I want the states to be blur bleeding into a stretch of road memories that feel like just a few short hours.

He slams the back door shut, really puts his arms and back into it and the car shakes as the door connects and bounces open again. 'It just has to get me home,' I hear myself whisper. The backpack, weathered by untold road and mountain miles, rests half on the seat, half suspended over the edge. He sits down and pulls his door shut, puts on his seatbelt and says "Chuck. Chuck Hobbs." He looks less than thirty. We shake hands; his hand is gritty and dry, the ridges of his palm and fingerprints severe, his grip and shake soft and passive. Chuck's stench is among the foulest known to man: a hint of sweat overpowered by wet-dog hair and a rotten, sour body odor which worsens when he spreads his legs.

"Merak Snyder. Where ya headed?"

"Hopefully Miami, in time. I'll go as far as you can take me today." Chuck's beard could conceal a frisbee, is knotted in places and adorned with burrs and dandelion umbrellas. His shirt is a red plaid flannel, jeans bare throughout but patched in places with random scraps of fabric from washcloths to burlap. On top of his head is a red "STP" cap with a mesh top.

"It's always the guys with the nasty cars who stop, you know? Once I'd like to ride in a Mercedes, or a Rolls, or something, but those guys have too much money to stop, or their time is too important, you know? Only people ever stop have cars like yours."

"You sound like you don't really want a ride."

"I didn't mean it like that, just observin' is all."

I start forward. The Nissan grinds in first gear and shakes when I steer it, pained sounds come through the floor and dash. The Nissan's own stink is no match for Chuck's.

"Sounds like your tranny needs fluid."

"This car has to get me back to Chicago, that's it. Selling it to some high schooler or scrap yard after that." I don't bother elaborating, even when he asks.

A phantom me next to a parked, blinking Colander stands at a guardrail enjoying phantom rain, looking into the canyon. I slow around the turn and take it all in; the trees, like lined soldiers, frame the right of the eel-like road but the central focus of the picture is a bridge with just inches of clearance above the river. I had expected to only ever pass this way once, this time is now the third I have passed it this direction. The memory of it seems to plan to stay here, making a home for the remains of Colander and the old me, the me who will never see Chicago again.

"Chicago? Nice city. Lived my first ten years there, then some in my twenties." Chuck takes his hat off and sets it on his knee, the bill to the floor. His dense hair is knotted like rigging. Wet-dog smell radiates like shockwaves. When he unbuttons his flannel, a too-small "Sailor Moon" in cracked silk screen letters above a picture of a skinny blonde cartoon girl with long pig tails shows his perfectly spherical belly. Chuck ages as I watch him, passing thirty then forty, stopping somewhere thereafter.

"Where did you live out there?"

"Familiar with Comiskey Park?"

"Been there a few times."

"How about the lakefront?"

"You mean near Navy Pier?"

"Sort of. Um, Union Station?"

"Never been. I actually live in the suburbs."

"Oh yeah? Which one?" He pulls a pack of gum from a pocket, puts a stick in his mouth and offers me one. I accept.

"Er, Lake Bluff." The gum is cinnamon tainted by Chuck funk.

"Merak Snyder of Lake Bluff. Thank you for giving me a ride."

"Figure I should. I've had to hitch a few times in the last couple weeks. But it wasn't me, though, someone else, you know?." The cinnamon gum changes the way my voice sounds to me, adding the wet, saliva sound of chewing to my words.

"Been a long few weeks?"

Chuck does not know. "Yeah. Yeah, it has been." The sound of chewing climbs through my jaw into my ear. It's squishy. Gum was never something my orthodontist allowed, so I never started chewing it. The wetness, burning taste, rancidity of this piece move between my teeth like slush through galosh treads.

The far edge of the road begins to narrow. Eroded, washed-out sections of dirt and road jut into it, only inches at first, but soon as much as three feet. The guardrail, where it has not collapsed into the river, either hangs from the road or is sway-backed, reaching into the void. The damage is new since yesterday.

We pass the place where I lost Colander. The guardrail is broken, dangling down the cliff for yards. Two cars' tire marks lead up to the edge and end.

Chuck sees this and whistles. "Well, whoever went over that's dead. Poor bastards."

"Yeah," I agree. "Poor bastard."

Before it becomes a conscious act, the car is braking hard. I can't let Chuck see the nice camera. "Hey, hold on. I gotta get some pictures of that." From inside the camera case I pull out the disposo-cam with the pictures left. When I shut the trunk, Chuck is outside the car and looking at me.

"Why you need pictures of that?"

"Well, you never know, could have some value to someone, or not. Either way, it's nothing to be concerned about. Just wait here."

The first shot is the way I approached, lined up neatly with the road and looking at the turn's blindness and the few thin hockey-stick trees that were once there. The second is as if I were in the Cadillac, at an inverse angle to the same area. The last is a picture of the drop from the road into the canyon, close as I feel safe getting, afraid the river will furor and a wave, like a grabbing hand, reach up and pull me and more of the road into it. When the third picture clicks the camera advances until the film is all spun together again and ready to be developed. The last pictures I'll keep in a frame on my wall. People will ask why I have pictures of a broken road on my wall. I'll smile, with half my face, nod and loose a single chuckle, and just tell them it was a place I once visited.

"What's the deal? You're treating this place like sacred ground. All quiet and walking slowly."

"If it is, then you talking would be blasphemous, right?"

"You're too serious, man. Let's get going. I don't like just sitting in one place. I'm like a shark, you know, I gotta keep moving or I die."

Back in the car so Chuck doesn't 'die,' I start telling him about my journey, the aspects that make it sound like a vacation. I embellish certain details, too, feeling a need to say things about Anna like 'she wanted me' and Kimberly, such as, 'yup, and I banged her.' Lying, though, feels like a clenching fist in my chest. Lying – flat-out lying – is just something that when it happens, I'll always be very aware of it. As I tell him these tales he hoots or says 'nice,' dragging on the 'I' like a skier riding a wide turn. I don't tell him about the vision, or my parents and my real reason for being here, or that I drove into that canyon.

Instead the trip is an 'expedition to see the country'; to which he says he's on one of those, too, and has been since he flunked outta high school. I explain how I began by driving the Interstates, but they're too fast: the scenery passes without the chance to be taken in, and the country just shrank. "Yes," I admit, "they're good for trucks and commerce and everything, but not for travel."

"I disagree."

"But travel is to see the country, not speed by it and get to a hotel or something. The joy is in the trip, not in the arrival."

"I see what you mean, but you're wrong."

"Whichever way it goes, you were hitching on a non-Interstate."

Chuck pauses. "True."

After a period of quiet because I do not want to tell the story a third time, I tell him about Watersharer. Silence is worse than re-telling something. She blows his mind. He keeps asking questions about her baldness, Jessup and how she talked to it, every aspect of the story he wants to hear twice. When I run out of facts I make some up. I make up her vision quests and expand on her take on music. Chuck isn't looking for truth, or any kind of universal human knowledge, he's looking for a tall tale, something he can use to make up his own. And in that sense, the story telling, lying, isn't lying, it's story-telling. As I story-tell I speed up, inadvertently. The excitement of the story, of the falsehoods and truths, translates into my foot.

"Whoa, man, slow it down. There's a cop back there," says Chuck.

I let my foot off the gas and cruise the Nissan back to the speed limit. A Chevrolet Caprice Classic follows a few car lengths behind. "How can you tell? 'Cause it's a Caprice?"

"Nah, brother. That Caprice's riding about three inches lower than a normal one, and it only has one guy. Cop cars have Corvette engines, and lots of extra gear. It makes them ride lower. Dead giveaway."

Chuck looks at the passenger's rear view and adjusts it slowly, calmly, so he can see behind us. "He's really staying back there."

"If he pulls us over no biggie. It's my ticket."

"If his lights go on, you floor it. No getting pulled over, no tickets, you floor it."

"Um, why?"

"Cops in this state are no good."

I don't like where Chuck is going – something bad is coming. "Not all cops are bad. I'm driving. If his lights go on, we do it my way."

Chuck looks at me, sideways through a knotted lank of hair that hangs off his left eye.

I keep driving at the speed limit and the light blue Caprice stays the same distance back. Chuck and I are quiet, watching it in the mirrors, waiting for lights or for it to leave. I slow down to five under and let it catch up, to see if it will pass. I chew with an open mouth, the sound comes at me from outside and in, now. The air I breath has a slight cinnamon/funk scent.

"Want it to pass?"

"Yeah. If you're right or not, no harm in him passing."

The Caprice stays behind us, watching. Bugs ping the windshield. Some splat, larger ones like cicadas or grasshoppers bounce away.

"Talk. Use your arms. Make it look natural," I say.

"About?"

"I don't care."

Chuck rambles. Recites lyrics from Beatles and Steppenwolf songs. Lists the ingredients in packaged cookies, but does so moving his arms, clapping in disgust, pointing at the palm of his hand and nodding or shaking his head. I nod, too.

The Caprice's turn signal goes on and it passes us. The driver is wearing a white shirt. The back seat of his car doesn't have a cage, there are not lights visible, nor a shotgun mounted on his dash and there are no antennas on the trunk or roof. "Look at that," I say, pointing out these things. "No cop has no extra antennas."

"Yeah, you may be right. I'm just jumpy around cops. I've had a few bad run-ins with them. Just keep it speed limit and we're good."

Yup, I saw this coming. "That's your business."

"It's all possession stuff. One assault."

"You don't have any drugs on you now, do you?"

"We could work out a trade, for the ride, if you want."

My jaw opens a bit and I stop chewing. "I shouldn't have asked." I spit the gum out, into the canyon. It's flavor had suddenly gone, except the Chuck taint.

"It's just a pound of pot, brother, nothing big. I'm taking it to some buddies in Minneapolis for some buddies in Sacramento. Don't sweat it. Just drive right and we'll be fine."

"Where does Miami fit in?"

"Down the road somewhere. More, bigger business. All of it none of yours."

We go on accompanied only by the ever-present sound of the wind charging through the car and tire tread smacking pavement. Chuck talks, occasionally, about the birch forests surrounding the road, how they suddenly changed from pine forests, the river we occasionally drive alongside or cross, the remaining hints of rain and occasional lightning strikes, idle observations such as "that's a lot of white trees" and "that one was bright." We pass a sign that says "Fatty's Truckers Dream Diner 6 miles"; Chuck reads it aloud. "Say," Chuck says. "I'm hungry for a real meal, how about you?"

"Why not."

‹◊›

Fatty's Truckers Dream Diner is a bad dream, the sort that follows you into real life and keeps you from feeling truly awake for a day; the sort of nightmare that creeps on the edge of your vision and the agents of which walk amongst the crowds you see and speak with the voices you hear.

The parking lot is full-up on trucks a crayon box of colors, a color-by-numbers of companies and logos. There are no lines for the parking spaces, no handicapped spot and no clear entrance or exit, no safety signs of any sort. The building is an ashlar square with a bowed roof. Behind it is a yellow, vinyl-sided rectangle with a large oval sign that says "Truck Wash" surrounded and throughed by pale blue water gushes. The parking lot wraps far behind the building. Signs behind the building say "Overnight parking $2.00 an hour", "Showers inside .80¢/gallon" and "Truck wash tokens sold inside." Painted on a railroad tie retaining wall are bright yellow arrows with black lettering "Truck Wash." I park next to the only other car in the lot, a police car.

"Whoa, man, maybe we shouldn't eat. I mean, I'm not so hungry now."

"Well, I am. And I'm driving. Grab your stuff."

Chuck looks at my spine as I turn to stand out of the car, and his eyes pierce through my clothes, skin and bones. As soon as I'm upright, I stretch every muscle I have. Push the arms up and left, out like a "T" and twist inches until my abdomen tells me to stop, lean slightly left and then right, kick my legs out a half foot or so until the jeans constrict my bruises too much.

"If you're sore from driving, I can take over when we get back."

As if. "I appreciate the offer, but no thanks. No matter how tired I get, I like driving. It gives me an opportunity to really see everything, because I have to pay attention." Chuck hefts his bag over his shoulder and starts walking inside. "And that's really what I'm here for, Chuck," I follow, "to see the country and really experience what it means to be American and free and all that." I stop because I almost laugh.

Past the doors' electronic beeping, the inside smells like various smokes and people stenches. Everything leaves a dirty streak when touched. To the left, in the restaurant section, is a low-hanging haze. In the right, a convenience store section, people stand and talk in front of a glass case filled with citizen band radios and walkie talkies. A counter serves warm sandwiches, fried chicken, more fried chicken, French fries and baked potatoes. Next to it is a cooler that wraps onto and across the next wall. Inside are cold sandwiches and staples like hot dogs and mayonnaise. The three aisles are labeled "Medicine and Jerky," "Chips, Dips, and Produce," and "Repair Equipment and Radios." In the corner, two police officers talk to a fat man with a pony tail, leather vest, green shirt, and black jeans. On a seat near them, another man, skinny and shaking, sits handcuffed with his hands behind his back, the chain through a slat on the chair back.

The men talk by a 'please wait to be seated' sign. It is black with white letters, in a brass frame.

The fat, pony-tailed man tells the officers that the skinny man owes him $46.23 for lunch and a shower. The skinny man does not look particularly clean, though.

"Got the money for that?" asks an officer.

The man shakes his head.

"Well, why'd you get the food and the shower if you couldn't afford it, Gary?"

The skinny man looks up at the officer. "I hadn't eaten in four days or showered in longer. I didn't want to. I had to."

"Excuse me," I say. "My name's Merak."

The fat man looks at me. "Fatty here. Marla will seat you in a minute."

"That's not it, I mean, I'll sit in time, but does he just need the money?" Chuck doesn't wait for Marla. There is an open booth near a window and a fire exit. He sits in it with his bag against the wall and watches us.

"Yes," says Fatty. "Not that it involves you." He adds the last part and looks at the officers as he says it.

I open my wallet and count my money. I pull out a fifty and set it on Gary's lap. "He's got the money."

"Now just a minute here," says Fatty. "I ain't takin' your money."

"Ain't my money," I say. "It's his. It's on his lap. Isn't that right, officers? I mean, If I give someone a gift, it's theirs then, right?" Chuck, looking down slightly, shakes his head and kneads his hands together.

"Technically, yes."

"He was still trying to rip me off."

As I turn to join Chuck, officer Granger puts his hand on my shoulder. "You sure you want to do this? This guy could be a killer or a rapist."

Gary's eyes are tired, life has treated him as second-class. The ones life chooses to treat well and the ones it treats badly do not make any sense to me; it just happens that way. I see in his eyes what was in Anna's when we sat in Colander as the sun set. The man's eyes match Michael's when I saw his trailer and inhaled. What's in Gary's eyes is also what was in Rachel's when Scott's wife brought the children in: a hope of some kind of better future. The kid's arms have no needle lines, his eyes are not bloodshot nor does he smell of alcohol. I look at a large, black menu with white tack-on lettering above the cash register. The right side of it says "to-go-go-go." Sandwiches are $3 each. I take my wallet back out. "You're right, officer." I drop six more dollars on his lap. "I'm not doing enough. He'd like a couple sandwiches to go, too, I imagine." After putting my wallet back I look at Officer Granger and say "If he were more than a kid who stole some stuff he'd be in your squad car. You know his name, after all."

Granger's eyes tell me I am right, though he doesn't nod or vocalize anything. He uncuffs the kid.

"I never been arrested before, I swear to you. I ain't never stoled nor nothing," says the kid, as he massages his wrists. He hands the money to Fatty, takes what change he gets, puts it and the sandwiches into his backpack, gladly. "Gary." He shakes my hand. "Thank you." I smile at him, and nod, and tell him to take care of himself. His handshake is strong, a man's handshake. It is not the doughiness of Chuck's.

Gary, tattered vinyl duffel over his shoulders, walks to the road.

"You've done your good deed for the day." Fatty walks off and back to the kitchen.

"He wasn't no rapist, just some confused, slow kid stuck alone. He lives in the mountains not too far from here. Never done no one wrong before." Officer Granger pats my back.

I nod and softly say 'thank you,' accepting this compliment is hard. The officers leave the restaurant.

When I join Chuck he already has a coke in front of him and his menu is closed. "It's good you didn't turn me in. You'd be an accessory. I'd have told them you were in on it. Jail'd destroy a punk shit like you. What kind of stupid thing was that, paying for that kid's food. He's gotta learn responsibility for his own self."

At the edge of the table is a small basket with ten sets of silverware rolled in napkins. It must be easier than bringing them out with each order. I take one and break the paper seal on the napkin, set the utensils out like my father taught me, and place the napkin to the side.

"Boy, you're just dumb. Best thing you coulda done was walk past them and sat right down with me. Woulda kept you from getting my wrath. I don't suggest you pull anything else like that because you don't want this trip getting . . . uncomfortable, do you? I can be a bad guest, believe me, buddy."

I take the menu and begin looking through it. It's a folded piece of legal-size paper, yellowed, stained with water drops, and frayed along the bottom.

"I don't gotta talk, nor be polite."

Mozza Logs are 2.99; Fried Jalapenos are 3.99.

"All this chit chat could end."

The menu lists eight different kinds of burgers plus a half page for a 'make-your own.'

"Don't make me get nasty, boy."

The hot dogs come in four sizes and three varieties. All with a side of chips and a twenty ounce pop for 2.50

"You listenin'?"

I turn the menu over and look at the beers and pops on draught. "I've smelled you, there is nothing nastier you can do to me."

"Don't place money on it."

"Know what you want?"

"Yeah."

"Good."

"Tell ya what, brother," Chuck says. "You been good to me this trip. I'll buy you lunch to say thank you. How'zat as an 'I'm sorry' for doggin' you out just now."

"Apology accepted."

I fold the menu in half and Chuck and I sit, looking outside, and Chuck makes occasional comments like "that's one fat bastard, Fatty is" or "She's not bad, if you take her face out of the equation." He points discretely with his elbow or a nod at almost every woman who walks through the doors or points to parked trucks he likes for their size, design, or general comfort.

The waitress takes our orders and looks at me. She is less than five feet tall with caring eyes and a thick, gray hair dome. "I don't know what you did to piss Fatty off. He told me to put eye drops in your drink and spit in your food. I ain't gonna, though. That fat asshole needs to be put in his place time to time."

"Thank you, ma'am."

"Call me Marla," she says, leaving.

"Visine, man. That'd give ya a bad case of the shits from here to Wednesday."

Actually, I want to say, Visine can cause organ failure and doesn't cause diarrhea. "Wednesday. Say, what day is it?"

"I dunno, that's just an expression."

Marla sets our appetizers on the table.

"I'm gonna hit the head right quick," he says. Chuck leaves his bag on the seat when he stands. Open it. I switch seats. Inside the duffel is a tightly balled green package about twice the size of a brick, wrapped in saran wrap and secured with mailing tape. It weighs a pound or so. There is a change of clothes, greasy and muddy, a few hundred dollar bills paper clipped together and a nickel-plated nine millimeter. The grip is walnut, the overall sheen so silver I stare back at myself from it; I look shocked, tired, dirty, beaten and ready for a long, long nap. The backpack sticks when it zips. I look up at the bathroom and see the door inch open. The zipper doesn't close. Marla walks up with our food.

"Shouldn't go through a man's stuff," she whispers. "Everyone in here's been watching you the whole time; ain't no good coming out of this."

I hold it open for her to see the pot and gun and when she does she looks out the window.

"Lovely afternoon, yessir, lots of clouds, even lighting, good drivin' weather, I've heard. Lovely indeed." She sets my burger in front of my seat and Chuck's double-stack quarter pounder with triple bacon, triple cheese, extra fries, and the larger bun in front of him. When Marla walks away I look back at the bathroom.

Chuck's flannel-clad arm pushes the door open. The bag's zipper is less than halfway closed. His head comes out the door but he stops, turns back to face the bathroom and talks to someone inside, laughing. The door closes and Chuck has gone back into the bathroom. The zipper is still stuck. I pull it back open, double checking that everything is packed as it was, and slowly, steadily pull the zipper closed. When Chuck walks out of the

bathroom I am back in my seat, sipping my pop empty and holding my
shaking hands under the table.

Chuck grabs his food and starts eating. He waves the waitress over.

"Hey, babe, did this guy here go rifling through my stuff while I was
shittin'?"

I hork pop through my nose. When it stops Marla takes the glass in
her hand. I hold a napkin under my nose.

"Darlin'," she says to Chuck, "If the inside of that bag smells like
you, then you'd need a hazmat suit to open it safely."

"You're not gunning for a big tip."

"If I expected tips, I'd not work here."

"Hey, while I got your ear, can you put five sandwiches, a case of
beer, a big bucket of fried chicken, biscuits, a large French fries, two
unopened boxes of beef jerky and, oh hell, a second case of beer on the tab?"

"Sure thing." Marla walks over to the convenience store and as she
rattles off the order the clerk there fills it and sets it by the cash register.

Chuck takes mastodonian bites from his burger and swallows after
chewing only twice. I eat the medium patty with mozzarella, mushrooms and
extra-thick tomato slowly. It isn't bad, but isn't anything I couldn't make
better at home with a skillet and toaster oven. Marla brings out a new pop for
me and tells Chuck his order is ready.

Fatty stands in the kitchen watching me eat. He leans on the side of a
steel fridge with his legs crossed at the knees, smiling. I drain half the glass
through the straw, wave, and hope Marla told the truth. He stops her and
points at me, his turned face shows his profile isn't bad, or ugly, but
spherical. She nods her head up and down then winks at me.

"How much money you got left on you?"

I stop chewing my burger and look at Chuck. A piece of gristle gets under my tongue. "Er, about enough for gas to Chicago, not any more. Why?"

"No reason." Chuck finishes eating mozza logs then orders three more sandwiches, two orders of fries and a case of pop for our trip.

When I finish my food, leaving the fries for later, I stand and tell Chuck I'll be right back. I walk over to the convenience store and wander the medicine and jerky aisle. It lives up to its name and is filled with twenty varieties of pep pills, various headache medications, some sleeping pills, dozens of gas and regularity remedies and at least ten kinds of heartburn relief. The impressiveness of the variety of over-the-counter fixes is rivaled only by the variety of beef jerky, turkey jerky, buffalo jerky, ostrich jerky, alligator jerky, and jerky/cheese mix packs. There are 'spicy,' 'hot,' 'extra spicy,' 'extra hot,' 'mild,' hickory smoked,' and 'flame-cured.'

Marla and Chuck wave to me, I wave back then walk into the bathroom. The bathroom is among the worst I have ever seen, except the showers. The shower stalls have solid gray doors with locks and digital keypads next to them. A hand-written sign taped to each door says "See cashier for access code." A naked man steps out of one and inside it is new shoes-white with a polished head and knobs and a soap and shampoo dispenser shaped as two breasts. The man turns and looks at me, his uncut penis hangs inches below his scrotum.

"If you want to earn yourself a free ride somewhere, gimme ten minutes to dress." The end of it begins to move upward and out of its poncho.

"Er, I got a car, but thanks."

He looks at me, licks his upper lip, and says "too bad for me." As an afterthought: "and you."

I turn and walk into the bathroom, glancing behind me to make sure he doesn't follow. Above each urinal are plastic cases that hold advertisements for the restaurant's convenience store section as well as various bail bondsmen. There is no soap and the only faucets are both missing the cold water knobs. I run my wet hands through my hair, fingers combing a part on the side.

At the table, Chuck, his food, and my fries are gone. The stack of beer cases, beef jerky, and fried chicken is gone from the convenience store counter. I ask Marla, as she busses the table, if Chuck left a tip.

"Hon," she says. "He said you were paying then he went out back and got in that truck." Marla points to a purple and white truck. The trailer says "Fluxx. Move in a state of Fluxx." It drives out of the rear of the parking lot, down an access ramp to the highway and away. I don't bother giving chase.

"Sigh. That shit figures. How much?"

"Fifty-eight dollars."

"What?" I yell. "Oh geez, I'm sorry. I didn't mean to yell."

"Ain't the first time I seen this, ain't the last. You're taking it pretty well."

"It's just money," I say, and keep saying as I hand Marla sixty-five dollars. "Thank you much."

"My pleasure. And don't you worry about nothin' – Fatty didn't get near your food."

I hand her another five and she takes it, smiling widely, and shoves it in her bra.

My car is cool, as is the afternoon. Truck engines rumble behind me like a machine choir. The clock on my dash says it is just after 1:30. I roll the windows down but don't start the car. I set my head against the steering wheel and my body begins to quake and I know that I can't hold it in for long. Cicada songs overpower all sounds but the trucks. I hook my hands on the bottom of the steering wheel, letting my elbows rest on my knees, pressing pain into my legs.

Crying begins with a single laugh-like sob. I do not cry because I'm scared but for everything which has happened to me: I didn't fall in love with Anna – Perhaps you should have; Watersharer; Michael – His life, his problems, his business; my visit with Grandfather – What did you expect to gain? Did you get it?; the vision – Don't forget Kimberly, maybe you should have fallen in love with her, too; the canyon – Which one? There were three; talking to my parents – especially talking to my parents – and now this. It has been a growing, strengthening movement and somehow I've lived though I shouldn't have. I should have died in Antelope Canyon and probably in the Grand Canyon, definitely in that river. And all I've come out of it with is a tender heel and a bruise-worked body. Something about that is unfair. Unfair to me an unfair to everyone else. Why have I constantly been spared?

After a time there is a knock on my car door. I sit upright, wiping my eyes, expecting to see Fatty kicking-ready to pull me from my car and bruise-coat my ass, or the naked man asking if I had car trouble and want a 'free' ride, but it is Marla.

"Everything okay?"

"Yeah, everything's fine." I wipe a hand under my eyes again, then sniffle.

"I saw you out here and wondered if this old kicker mighta died. It'd fit with your day."

"Marla, you have no idea, believe me."

"Stay strong. You'll do alright. I promise."

"Thank you, Marla." The thank you comes easily this time and I sob once more with it. Once more for the road. The Nissan starts easily, the engine whines lightly, transmission grinding as I back out and accelerate down the ramp to the road. The same ramp which Chuck just ran down, the same road. I get the idea to chase them down, cut them off, slam on my brakes and beat chuck's head to a mash with my tire iron, but then I remember his nickel nine millimeter.

The grind lessens in second gear, but is there. The driving is leisurely. I use the time to calm myself. The road here is not washed away. The guardrails are intact, even new, and the hills solid. The mountains' white- and gray-treed forest on the sides of the highway pass like a long series of hatch marks. Each one could be for a blessing I've had in my life.

‹◊›

About a thousand miles east, my parents are at home, probably getting ready for dinner. They are holding hands and saying grace like they have every night for the last eighteen years. After the regular "God is great; God is good; we thank him for our food," they would each add a blessing for the day. "Thank you, God, for keeping Merak alive through everything he has been through," my mother might say. "Thank you, God, for saving him for me to kill," my father would joke in response then add, in earnest, "Thank you, God, for watching over Merak."

"Thank you, God, for sparing me from that river, from Chuck, from the naked man, from falling in love with Anna or Kimberly, and from the other dangers I am forgetting or unaware of," I say, joining in their prayer because space cannot unite us right now.

Mother may have cooked something, but more likely got carry out from a restaurant. There is a whole chicken on the table sided by mashed potatoes and gravy, spirals and cheese, and two slices of hot apple pie.

They may be talking, coming to some better understanding of each other and the nearly two decades they've put themselves through, having the sort of fight children sit on the stairs and listen to. Maybe they will come to an understanding. Maybe they love each other, but not likely – things like that don't happen in real life. Tonight could be the first night they've talked easily in weeks. They know that I'm safe, that I'm coming home; the years of anger are aired. They have these reliefs and more than a quickly written note.

Ahead, red and blue lights flash. They come from a light blue Caprice which sits behind a stopped red Firebird. A man in a white shirt is talking to the driver of the Firebird, who nods and seems apologetic.

The road continues on, soon it is again paralleled by the river I fell into, though at a far more distant place. As the road again draws near the canyon, here much shallower and friendlier, though still rain-stuffed, my ears pop and insects begin hitting the windshield in force. Most are grasshoppers that bounce off without leaving too much of a mark, but some explode leaving long stretches of bug splat. And then a dragonfly hits, leaving a large, colorful teardrop in its wake. It looks rather like modern art, or a spilled tray of condiments.

The engine whine, which had been a constant sort of white noise, grows to a shrill racket. It is like a feral cat in heat, or a pager going off during a movie: it is an unrequested, unwanted, and unneeded intruder. I slow down, and the sound calms but then gets louder, more insistent, more needing of companionship or attention.

Smoke, thin tendrils of it, comes through the vents. It is thin like shower steam, but smells like a semi-truck slamming on its brakes. The smoke curls in the compartment then is shattered by the wind coming through the car. The Nissan drifts over the rumble strips alongside the road, repeatedly, as I look at the vents and ask "what now? What's going to go wrong next?"

I shut the vents and slow down more. The needle is just past thirty-five. There have been no cars since the Caprice and Firebird. No trucks, no one. The road is thinner, the lanes narrower, and I must have missed my turn to go back to Denver. I hope Wyoming is nice this time of year because that's where it looks like I'm headed – if my car would stop smoking.

Smoke steals through the closed slits, and this time it is black and rancid. It smells like a mouse left to jucify a beer can. My nose burns and I sneeze uncontrollably, hitting the accelerator as I do, sending in thicker plumes of smoke.

From under the hood a thin, wide sheet of smoke spills out and over my car, then from the hood's edges. I reach behind the steering wheel and put the car in neutral, turn the engine off, and let it coast to a stop. I park it and get out, taking my camera and tool kit from the trunk and walking twenty feet away from the car. Inside the red metal tool kit is a complete mechanic's set. All of it Craftsman, Metric and Standard rule, every piece of equipment needed for any repair. All of it would help if I'd listened to my father when he tried to teach me how to fix a car.

The pieces are horribly out of order and I open all the drawers and the top compartment, unfolding inner trays as it spreads, and empty the box. I organize all the pieces by rule, placing metric on my left. Then shape, the long tubish pieces get lined up and the short stubbers get grouped, too. Then by size from the smallest hex head to the largest. The three rachets I organize by size. There is a small tack hammer and rubber mallet which I set separately. I will never use any of it. Two empty slots in the case tell me pieces are missing, a seven inch extender and a long, ten-millimeter tubish thing. The set looks unused, however. No fingerprints, no grease, neither dirt nor signs of wear. My dad may like it, though it isn't as nice as his set, which is in a wheeled case.

I shut the toolbox and close the clasps, sit on my camera case and watch smoke come up from my car like a wide, billowing flag to be spirited away by the wind.

On the far side of the road the river calls to me. It is a wide, lazy stretch of water with small rocky islands throughout. The water is clear and fish swim in it. On the far side is a wood house with a boat launch. Two small rowboats are tied to the dock. One has an outboard mounted in the back, the propeller up. The river seems to offer a truce, but I don't go near it, favoring the idea of waiting for a car. With luck, the blue Caprice will show.

After an hour no cars have approached, no one from the house has come out to see if I need help, and I have slapped dead countless small insects that landed on me. I walk to the car, which still looses thin lines of smoke, and pop the hood. When I do, smoke mushrooms up from it. Parts of my engine are like an ash pit. I put my camera and tools back in the trunk and start the engine. It turns over, but I kill it just in case.

There is the sound of crickets, and cicadas. Various birds do their thing, but nowhere do tires meet pavement. I reopen my trunk and then the camera case. I put the 30-80mm lens on and hang the strap around my neck. The two remaining unused rolls of film I put in my back pocket.

A fly fisherman has taken to the river, but doesn't see me. I decide not to go near the water – the clear, living, talking river – fearing it wants me still. I take pictures of the fisherman as he waves his rod above the river like a magic wand, weaving the spell which will land him a dinner-worthy trout. Back and forth with a hint of spinning. Through the lens, fish eat insects on the water surface. The ripples spread like kindnesses.

Next to me is the birch forest on a slight incline. The shield of gray, ultimately supplicant to the sun, passed and the sky is a pale blue with high, thin clouds. Trees from the far side of the road cast their shadows toward the more heavily forested side, longingly, mournfully, perhaps wishing to join their brethren across the road. I do what they cannot.

Inside the forest sounds change, as do the smells. The road smelled of tar and my engine. The forest smells of ground cover, decomposition and trees decades long on their sides, and the occasional pines scattered amongst the white and gray of the birch and aspen. It smells of the mosses and ferns that grow on the trees and the short grass on the forest floor. Above me a squirrel glides from the end of his limb to another. Water shakes from the leaves onto me as he does. The squirrel takes a twig and drops it at me, then seems to chuckle. The birches are smooth, welcoming. They are tactile plants and seem to have something to say cutaneously as their arm branches and fingertip leaves reach down and brush my hair. They stand before me, bare, revealed, telling me to join them. They will be put in my photo album to be remembered later as they are now.

Sunlight percolates through the leaves, moving along the forest floor in backs and forths as tree tops sway. Perhaps when the pictures are developed the light will look like water on the leaves. Perhaps not. I'm not the photographer I once dreamed I could become. I take off my camera and set it on a stump. My shirt is next and I hang it on a broken branch. The air is cooler here than on the road. Water hits my bare back and gooseflesh pops up all over. My shoes I take off then stuff my socks into them. The moss under my feet is soft, deeper than my toes and it curls over the tops of them. There are mushrooms scattered throughout it. I undo my belt and slide my pants and boxers off at once. Individual spots of sun touch me and are calm, passionate. They tell me to grab my things and follow.

Between trees lies a deer trail. "Go left." The voice carries in it command and comfort but also sadness, like a parent whose child has just ridden his bike without training wheels, tasting for the first time their ability to leave, becoming intoxicated on freedom. It still sounds like it smiles, though. It knew what I would and would not do and perhaps every event, every direction was meant ultimately to lead me to this forest.

The canopy lives in the wind. My grandfather must have had a similar experience, some moment with nature, that made him decide to stay in Arizona after he knew he would never marry that Indian girl. Certainly, there was a defining moment for my father in Chicago, one which made him stay here. The skyline, perhaps. The opportunities for an architect, possibly. Fishing on Lake Michigan, maybe. A girl, most likely. Maybe my mother. What will I do because of women? I didn't stay in Arizona; I didn't think of staying with Kimberly. Maybe my father is right. It is up to me to break this tradition. Maybe I even can.

The deer trail leads to an oblong opening with peninsulas of forest reaching into it. Here the trees are different. Bark has been stripped at the bottoms and the knots are black. The trees still sway and the path leads down the clearing toward an opening, more a tunnel, in the trees. The voice says "follow," whispers it to me with the wind from across the clearing.

The grass is cool, warm, and tall. Seeding ends reach out to me and I let them pass through my free hand. The tunnel is not long and soon I can see the end lets out to a small lake. By the forest is an abandoned wheel. It is nearly my height, metal, browned with rust, and supported at an angle by a broken axle. Next to it are parts of an old harness, a ploughshare, and the remains of a molding board. The lake is no more than an acre of clear water where pan fish dart along the shore. Around it are pine trees, more so than at other places in the forest, and they're larger. The wind from behind the pines smells light, free, filtered.

I lean against the wheel, rusted to a richly textured brown, making sure nothing except my arms touch it. Short grasses and bushes surround me and far off, ten miles or more, is an interstate and a small town. Apartment complexes, condominiums, and hotels chessboard the side of a mountain.

I fold my clothes, set them on the ground as a pillow. In the lake two ducks splash as they land. Grass nestles into my back and I put my hands behind my head, close my eyes and enjoy the feel of the sun on my body.

East is Deer Lake; dogs are being walked; the usual winners win this evening, too. Rick, Amy, and my other friends have heard I am all right and are at Denny's talking, joking freely for the first time in weeks. Or they are at Rick's house playing video games, eating pizza and hitting the basement beer fridge. They wait for me. But, in a way, they will be disappointed

It is clear: There are two of me, now. One will stay behind, wander the west and continue to look for answers he cannot find. The other will go back to Chicago, more home now than before. I see Chicago as if I stood at a distance and looked at the skyline. Clouds float between skyscrapers like yarn on a loom. The red, blinking lights of the buildings' antennas barely visible through the ceiling. The lake is choppy at the shore but out a distance are the white triangles of ships' sails. Along the shore people walk, listening to the waves and getting to know each other and themselves better. There is where I will face my parents, confront the future, and do what I can to change everything that has yet to happen.

41542148R00116